Passage of Time
A Novel

Sissy de Grace

Passage of Time

A Novel

Sissy de Grace

Dog Tag Publishing

Crawford, Nebraska
in collaboration with Lulu Enterprises INC.

DogTag Publishing
Crawford, Nebraska

Publisher: Juliet Freitag

Editors:

Kelly Regan-Phillips   E. Franklin
Anna Lee   Juliet Freitag

Publisher's Note:

This is a work of fiction. All characters and incidents are the product of the author's imagination, places are used fictitiously, and any resemblance to actual person, living or dead is entirely coincidental.

LOC Control Number: 2005937288
ISBN: 1-4116-5717-9

First printing November 2005

publisher/editors may be contacted through:
www.dogtagpublishing.com
publisher@dogtagpublishing.com
Sissy can be contacted at: sissydegrace@yahoo.com
Front and back cover photos taken at Chadron State Park
by Juliet Freitag, Copyright© 2005

Dedication:

To my mother who encouraged me to write, and to see the world in non-traditional ways.

Acknowledgements

As with any book, there are many, many people behind the scenes who make it possible. First, I would like to thank my editors Kelly Regan-Phillips, Diane Clark, Juliet Freitag, E. Franklin, and Anna Lee, who took the time to read and reread through this story, making it the best possible. Especially to Kelly, who had just had a baby, and found time between working and baby-care to not only catch my mistakes, but encourage the inspiration behind the words! Also to DogTag Publishing for making this book a reality.

I would also like to take the time to thank my family, for understanding that writing isn't just something I do, it's something I am.

Thank you to Wayne Kelly from the Chadron State Park, for answering all my obscure questions, right before closing up shop for the night. Thank you to Charlene Savage, and Chadron State Park, for all your help! Front cover and back photos are from Chadron State Park.

Thank you to Lori Frederick at Pine Ridge Garden Center, for allowing me to take pictures around the nursery and greenhouses.

Thank you to Susan, Tony, Mary, and all of the other friends who encouraged me along the way.

To my dear friends Jenny Gettino, Roxanne Stewart-Black, Kelly Regan-Phillips, Vicky Rodriguez, the Windler sisters, and to Wendy and Lenora, for being friends of a very unique kind, and the type of women characters are made of. I am extremely fortunate to have you all in my life!

Sissy de Grace

Chapter One

The first time she met him, he was a skinny ten-year-old boy. Had Genevieve known then, the journey their lives would take, and how their paths would cross again, she might have paid more attention to that first meeting. She didn't though. She was a young bride of twenty-three, with a five-month-old baby on her hip, and dinner to think about, when the light tapping came at her door. She opened it, and looked into the face of a grubby little boy. His expression was worn, and he had the serious face of a person who is much older than they look. He regarded her closely, his intense sky-blue eyes peering out from under his baseball cap. A shudder passed through her, looking at those eyes, which seemed much too large for the boy's head.

"Do you want your lawn mowed?" he asked bluntly, never taking his eyes off hers.

She shifted the baby, Becca, to her other hip, and eyed him carefully. The boy's shirt was thin and filthy, and his legs were covered with bruises. He hardly looked big enough to push the lawn mower he was dragging behind him. Genevieve bit her lower lip, considering his offer.

The lawn *was* overgrown with weeds. Her husband, Joe, wouldn't be able to get to it before the week was out. His construction business was taking off, and he was usually at the site until well after dark. She wanted to get out and tend the yard, but with the house and baby to take care of, it felt like she didn't even have time to shower, much less mow the lawn. The neighbors hadn't started complaining yet, but she had seen the expression on their faces, as they walked out to their cars. Before long, she expected a weed notice posted to her door by the town, if things kept up at this rate. A scrawny kid to mow it was better than nobody at all.

"How much?" she finally asked.

"Five dollars, and a glass of something to drink about half-way through," the boy replied simply, shifting eagerly from one foot to the other.

He waited quietly while she made up her mind, scratching his chin, which was coated in a layer of dust. His fingernails left clean streaks, where he had scratched the dirt away.

Genevieve smiled inwardly at the boy's candor. He seemed so mature for such a small guy, and she wondered just how old he really was. He gazed out at the lawn, which was nothing more than weeds and dirt, and then back at her expectantly. She nodded her head and he nodded back—an unspoken agreement. He silently turned, pushing the large mower out into the yard.

All of a sudden, Genevieve felt bad, because she knew the yard would be horrible to mow—being so overgrown. She started to call out to the boy, but stopped herself short, knowing he would be offended if she even suggested such a thing. She slowly shut the door, as she heard the mower fire up. Later, she couldn't resist peering out of the window to see if he could really push the mower through the weeds. He strained and struggled, as the dust blew up all around him, but, damn, if he wasn't actually doing it!

Genevieve shook her head, and let the curtain fall back into place. Becca gurgled from her highchair, slinging peas onto the floor. Genevieve sighed and grabbed the dishrag, as another spoonful of peas hit the wall.

About an hour later, the mower stopped, and Genevieve heard footsteps come up to the door. She opened the door, just as his hand was raised to knock. He lowered his hand shyly, and stuck it in his pocket. His head was down, waiting for her to say something. Lines of sweat trickled down his dusty face, making Genevieve feel even worse about agreeing to let him mow the lawn. She noticed how bony his legs were in his shorts, and decided cookies might be in order as well.

"Would you like that glass of lemonade now?" Genevieve asked.

He scuffed his shoe against the worn floorboards of the porch, and bobbed his head up and down. He made no inclination to move, so she knew she'd have to nudge him along.

"Well, come in then!" Genevieve said, laughing softly.

The boy's head snapped up and he peeked quickly around, shocked that she would invite him into her home. He almost looked like he would run away, so she put her hand on his arm and led him in to the house. He came along without a fight, his eyes glancing around at the tidy living room. He rubbed his nose, and adjusted his baseball cap. Genevieve silently questioned when the last time he had had a bath was. She had never seen him around the neighborhood. It was a shame his parents didn't take better care of him. He seemed like such a good kid.

"I don't bite, you know," she said, teasing. "What's your name?"

"Danny," the boy answered. He sat down at the kitchen table, but only after she motioned it was okay.

Genevieve poured two glasses of lemonade, and put out a plate of peanut butter cookies. She sat down across from him, pushing the plate towards him. He stared at the plate hungrily, seeming unsure as whether or not to take a cookie. She smiled and pushed the plate a little closer. After a moment, he tentatively reached out to take one, devouring it in seconds. Genevieve handed him another, which he took and nibbled on bashfully.

"Well, Danny, you sure are a hard worker! How old are you, anyway?"

"Thank you, Mrs. Howard. I'm ten, but I'll be eleven next week," Danny replied. He grinned, revealing a row of beautiful white teeth.

Genevieve noticed how smiling lightened up his whole face. He pulled off his baseball cap and rubbed his head, making his curly, white-blond hair stick up in every direction, with sweat and grime. He placed his cap back on his head, and gulped the last of his drink. Genevieve wanted to know more about him, but he rose quickly and looked towards the front door.

"I'll go finish now. Thank you for the lemonade."

"Wait! Let me pay you now, in case the baby goes down for a nap. This way, you won't have to knock on the door again," Genevieve said, jumping up to grab her purse, before he disappeared out the door. She reached in, pulling out a ten dollar bill.

"Mrs. Howard, I don't have change," Danny whispered, his face turning red.

Genevieve felt ashamed for his embarrassment, but knew the money was more needed in his hands, than in hers. She patted his shoulder and smiled. She wondered if she should know him, since he kept calling her by her name. But of course, the name was on the mailbox! It was as simple as that.

"Oh, don't worry about it. That's all I have, so keep it. And call me Genevieve, please."

Danny stood staring at her, for what seemed quite a time, his blue eyes never blinking. Then he turned without saying a word, and walked out the door—the ten dollar bill still clasped tightly in his hand.

She heard the mower start up again, just as the baby started to cry. She scooped Becca up off the blanket she had been playing on, and walked over to the window. Becca curled her fists tightly in Genevieve's long auburn hair, and blew raspberries in the air. Genevieve hugged Becca tight against her, a subconscious need to protect her. Becca whined and pushed away, a conscious need to be independent.

Genevieve watched the boy, struggling to push the mower through the tall grass, and remembered when she was that age. Her own shyness had kept her from really opening up to people, other than her grandma. Even her parents had seemed distant to her growing up... strangers. If it hadn't been for having her grandma so close, she practically would have raised herself. Outside her grandma's doors, she had been such a loner, and terribly insecure about her presence in the world.

Perhaps, that was why she had been attracted to Joe

when she was eighteen. He was fourteen years older than her, and seemed to have it so together. Genevieve was newly out on her own, working her first real job as a waitress at the coffee shop. Joe came in every day of the week, from his construction job, for lunch. She thought Joe was so handsome, with his light brown hair, with just a touch of gray. *Distinguished*, she thought, *mature*. He would watch her all the time, but never said anything more than his order. She figured he just wasn't interested in a young girl like herself.

Almost two years went by, with him coming in, watching her, and saying his order. Finally, one day he came up to her, as his co-workers were leaving, and stopped her by the bathrooms. She thought she was in his way and tried to move, but he placed his hand on her arm and met her eyes. Genevieve couldn't believe a man like him would give her the time of day. That day he asked her to the movies, and she happily said yes.

For a year they dated, and then he popped the question on her twenty-first birthday, even though he was thirty-five years old. She had said yes immediately, totally enamored with the thought of being taken care of by Joe.

Six months later, they were married in a lavish ceremony, with all of Joe's friends in attendance. Not too many people showed up Genevieve knew, but she had thought in time Joe's friends would become her friends too. Her mother had sent a card, but her grandma was too ill to see Genevieve get married, much to both of their distress. Genevieve sucked it up, and reminded herself that she would pull through, just like she always had. But it had hurt. She leaned on Joe for support, and he happily filled the role of her everything, for the time being. Becca was born when Genevieve was twenty-three, and their marriage everything she could have hoped for.

Becca's fussing pulled Genevieve out of her thoughts, and she realized it was past the baby's naptime. She took Becca upstairs, and laid her in her crib. She sat down in the rocking chair beside the crib, and started to sing a lullaby. Becca gurgled and played with her toes. After a few minutes, she started to doze off.

Genevieve put her head back wearily, and closed her eyes. *Just a minute, to catch my second wind.* Her mind thought about trivial things, like dinner and the laundry. Her feet kept a steady rhythm, rocking back and forth, back and forth. When she opened her eyes, the room was dark, and she realized she had fallen asleep. It was getting past dinner time. She hopped up, peering into the baby's crib. Becca was still sleeping soundly, her thumb plugged into her mouth. Genevieve laid the blanket Becca had kicked off back over her legs, and touched the baby's soft arm. Becca smiled in her sleep, and kicked the blanket back off again. Genevieve sighed, smiling to herself in acceptance of defeat.

Genevieve peeked out the window, to see the lawn was mowed. The boy, Danny, was gone. She was sorry she hadn't gotten to say good-bye, or learn more about him. He seemed to be carrying a burden, too big for someone so young. His eyes revealed an old soul, and even though he was a child, Genevieve felt she had been in the presence of someone her own age.

She hoped she hadn't offended him, by giving him more money than agreed upon. She didn't know where he came from, or what his story was, but she saw the way he clutched the money. She knew, even though she did have a five dollar bill in her purse she could have given him, she had done the right thing.

Chapter Two

Life goes on, people change. There is nothing like watching a child, especially an only child, go off to kindergarten on their first day of school, to make a mother think about the future, and her place in it.

By the time Becca started kindergarten, Genevieve craved for something more than just taking care of the house, and making sure hot meals were on the table every night. She watched her little girl start to learn and grow away from her, and recognized her own spirit needed tending, too. Joe headed out every morning for work, with a kiss and a smile, while Becca ran out to meet her friends on their way to school. Each went off to a life, which Genevieve was not part of.

After they both left for the day, Genevieve would sit at

the dining room table quietly, with a cup of coffee, and just think. Sometimes, it was about things she had to do that day, but other times it was remembering the dreams she had as a girl. To grow up, and be this or that. To go here or there. It left her feeling sad and alone. Genevieve was grateful for the life she had, but she still wondered if there was something waiting for her outside the doors of their quaint little home. Something which was meant for her alone.

One cool October morning, after Joe had left, and Genevieve had seen Becca off at the door, she stopped at the mirror in the front hallway. She turned her head slightly each way, taking in her reflection. Her gray eyes still sparkled with flecks of green, just as they had when she was first becoming a woman. Her light auburn hair had not a hint of gray, and its waves cascaded gently over her shoulders. At twenty-nine, her skin still showed no real signs of aging, although dark circles did shadow her eyes.

I am still young, and already giving up on my dreams for my life.

Determined by that revelation, Genevieve went into the living room, to dig through the stack of newspapers Joe had left by the fireplace. She scanned through, until she found the listings for the local college.

Maybe a course to stimulate her mind. Maybe just a few classes to remember who she was, who she wanted to be.

She came across the listings for the following winter, and picked a few classes that seemed interesting. A shot of exhilaration shot through her body, as she let her mind grasp on the possibilities. As a young girl, living in her hometown of Chadron, she had watched the college kids arrive every fall, thinking eventually one day she would become one of them. Well, that was until she met Joe.

Joe had moved to Chadron, Nebraska from Arizona, when a construction job had opened up in the area. He often traveled to different places for work, but always returned home to Arizona after the job was complete. Until he came to Chadron. Once here, he had fallen in love with the beauty of the northwest Nebraska area. He had joked with Genevieve often, that it was much different than the cowboys and corn he had expected to see when he arrived. The massive buttes and the pine ridge had taken his breath away, and when he met Genevieve, he vowed to stay in Chadron forever.

His parents, now much older, were still in Arizona, and had never traveled to Nebraska to see them. They blamed the cold, the drive, and their age, but Genevieve always suspected it was because Joe had married someone so much younger than himself. As it was, he was the youngest of three children, and the others had all settled somewhere in the southwest. All of their own children were already grown. His siblings never had made any attempts to have a relationship with Joe and Genevieve. Joe was more than willing to say good-bye to his life in Arizona, and had not once expressed a desire to see his family, or go back there.

Genevieve, on the other hand, had been born at Chadron Community Hospital, and had never left the town. She'd attended the schools, shopped in the stores, and knew the streets like the back of her hand. Her parents had traveled often, during her childhood, seeking bigger and greater things, but even as a child Genevieve was content to rock on her grandmother's front porch, watching the birds fly overhead. She had spent most of her childhood with her grandma, and felt it had made her a richer person for it.

Even then, she knew Chadron was her home. Chadron had everything she had ever wanted, including the college. Now, with the idea looming in front of her, of finally becoming one of those students she would watch as a child, she knew it was time to make that dream a reality.

She worried what Joe would think. He was an old-fashioned man, and made enough money in construction to make a good life for them. He wasn't one to rock the boat, and didn't like change. Would he think she was being silly, or even selfish?

She didn't care; she wanted to feel whole again! She had the rest of her life to think about. Becca was in school now, and the house needed little tending with no babies around anymore. Genevieve was ready for a new page in her story. In her heart, she knew Joe would be supportive, no matter what he felt, because that was his nature. Even when they didn't agree at times, he never belittled her or negated her feelings.

When Joe got home that night, Genevieve had dinner ready, and was sitting at the table with the newspaper. Her hands shook slightly, sweating profusely, as she fingered a corner of the page. Becca had come home earlier from school, and was upstairs playing dress-up, with some of Genevieve's old clothes. Joe came in, set his case down, and gave her one of his winning smiles.

"Hey, sweets! Dinner smells good!" He leaned over and kissed her firmly on the mouth, his lips warm from the day.

Genevieve relaxed, feeling his whiskers tickling her chin. After all, this was Joe—her husband, her friend. She looked up at him, and admired his still fit physique. He met her eyes; his golden-hazel eyes twinkling softly back at her.

"It's Shepherd's Pie, your favorite. I wanted to eat a little early, so we would have some time together tonight," she said, slightly breathless, the heat between them apparent.

Becca raced into the room, her long golden-brown hair

whipping behind her, and into her dad's arms. He swooped her up, kissing her on the cheek. She wrapped her small arms around his head, and kissed his nose.

"Now, there's my girl! Learn a lot at school, did you?" Joe asked, tickling her tummy.

Becca giggled and nodded.

"Mrs. Freeland says I'm a good napper. We had cookies and juice!"

She squirmed out of Joe's arms, darting out of the room, as quickly as she had come in. Everything in a five-year-old's world seemed to be in broken fragments, which had no need to connect or make sense.

"You wash up, Bec! Mom's got our favorite for dinner tonight!" Joe yelled after her, laughing. He glanced over at Genevieve and winked. "She's something, isn't she?"

Genevieve chuckled and stood up to pour some tea, the newspaper laid aside temporarily forgotten. When everyone sat down to dinner, she saw the paper sitting on the chair beside her, and remembered that she wanted to talk to Joe about taking some courses at the college.

She looked around the table at her husband and her child, happily chattering away about their days. Was she being too greedy to want more? Joe was a loving husband and a kind father. Becca was an easy-going child who made her smile. It wasn't that they weren't enough though; it was that taking care of other people wasn't enough to stimulate Genevieve inside.

After dinner was done, and the dishes cleared, Genevieve joined them in the living room. Becca was coloring a picture of a giant green kitten eating grapes, or some other round objects—only Becca really knew. Joe was reading the daily paper; his glasses perched on the tip of his nose. Genevieve sat down with the college listings on her knee, and cleared her throat nervously. Joe peered over his glasses and smiled, the corner of his eyes crinkling up.

"What you got there, hon? Reading the paper?" he asked, looking at the papers folded on her lap.

Genevieve cleared her throat again, and glanced down at the listings.

"Well, Joe, I wanted to talk to you about something. Just an idea I had," she stammered, and then went on, "with Becca in school now, I have some free time, and I was thinking about taking some courses over at the college."

Joe watched her expressionless for a moment, and then raised his eyebrows, "I had no idea you wanted to go to college! Aren't you a bit old for that? I mean, not that you're really old, but wouldn't you feel out of place with all those eighteen-year-olds?"

Genevieve knew Joe would not truly understand. He saw no need for college himself, since his construction business brought in more money than most college-educated people did in Chadron. She knew she had to show it to him in a way he could appreciate. Even if it took a bit of guilt.

"Well, Joe, when I first met you, I was really just a girl, and we married so soon after. I didn't know what I wanted to do then. Nor do I for sure now, but I do know I want to explore and see what's out there. It would make me happy."

Joe nodded slowly, as he ran his hands through his graying hair. He understood wanting to be happy in life, seeking out things that made it worth getting up in the morning. Genevieve's happiness was important to him. He was a man who loved his job and his family, and he knew Genevieve loved the family, but could see her wanting something for herself. He couldn't honestly understand her desire to sit in a classroom with young kids, but he loved Genevieve, and couldn't see any harm in her taking a few classes.

Sometimes, Joe felt bad that he married Genevieve when she was so young, since he had lived a lot of life before then, and was ready to settle down. He just didn't want to wait once he met her, she captivated him. He had been afraid if he waited, she would have disappeared out of his life forever. Hell, it took him two years just to get up the nerve to ask her out back then! He got up and walked over to her, leaning in close, to where he could feel her breath on his neck. He kissed her on the forehead.

"Hon, if it makes you happy, it makes me happy," he said.

His heart filled when he saw her eyes shine. This was something he could give her back. In turn, the joy he saw in her face paid him back immeasurably.

"Thank you, Joe! I just knew you would understand. I love you so much! " Genevieve cried, as she leapt up.

She wrapped her arms around him snugly, sighing with relief. Joe buried his face in her soft hair, and put his arms around her shoulders.

Becca regarded them quietly, her hazel-green eyes sparkling in the firelight. She smiled at the sight of her parents in each others arms. She bent her head back to her coloring, and beamed with contentment.

For the rest of her life, Becca would remember this exact moment, and knew that when she grew up and got married, she wanted it to be just like that.

Chapter Three

College *had* made a difference in Genevieve's life. When she walked those halls, Genevieve felt like somebody making their mark on the world. Not just a mom, not just a wife, but an intelligent strong woman, whose opinions mattered.

She had never felt like that in high school. There, she had kept her head down, feeling like an awkward outcast. Being smart then had made her be pushed aside by the other kids. She hadn't played sports, hadn't been voted homecoming queen, and hadn't been asked out on dates... or even to the prom.

In college, even though she still felt shy and vulnerable, her intelligence shined, which other students and professors valued above everything else. College was more about what one knew, rather than who one knew. But still…

Sixteen months into taking college classes, Genevieve still didn't know where it was taking her. She hadn't decided on a field of study, and now the classes seemed fragmented and purposeless. She was consistently on the Dean's list, but it never felt like she was moving forward. She felt like she was just running in place.

What she needed was a path. A place to go, a goal to strive for. Genevieve had to decide on a major, to make continuing on worth her time and their money. She knew it had to be something she believed in.

Genevieve sat on a bench outside the cafeteria, and closed her eyes. What did she love? What was important to her? Why had she wanted to come to college? Who did she want to be? She opened her eyes slightly, letting the shadows of the leaves on the trees dance around in the sunlight, in the slits of her eyes, as she let her mind slip back to an earlier time in her life.

An image of herself, as a child picking flowers behind her grandma's house, sprang to mind. She was barefoot, covered in dirt, and happier than she had ever been. She had spent hours playing in Grandma's garden, watching the insects, pulling the weeds, gathering flowers and vegetables. Sometimes, Grandma would be alongside her, and they would work silently tending the garden. Occasionally, Grandma would hum a tune, while Genevieve tried to figure out what the song was.

There was no place Genevieve would have rather been, than by her grandma's side, back in the garden. When they were done, Genevieve didn't want to wash her hands, because they smelled of the dirt—fresh and earthy.

Grandma always said, "Come now, Genny, there's always more dirt for tomorrow. It'll be right here waiting on you."

That was it! Genevieve came out of her memories of the past, and jumped to her feet, startling a flock of birds resting in the nearby trees. Students walking into the cafeteria stopped, surprised, and stared at her. She shielded the sun from her eyes, embarrassed at the attention she had drawn to herself, and smiled shyly.

"Oh, I'm sorry, I was just… I mean, I just decided on my major," she sputtered out.

One of the guys gave her a thumbs-up with a grin, and the girl next to him smiled sweetly, taking his hand. They turned and kept walking, when the boy stopped suddenly. He turned back to Genevieve, a look of curiosity crossing his face.

"Don't hold us in suspense," he said, chuckling. "Well, what is it?"

"Oh, um… it's Horticulture," Genevieve said, her face feeling hot, but her heart full of pride.

The boy nodded his head slightly, and smiled at her. Then he disappeared quickly into the cafeteria.

All of a sudden, it all fit. All the months of struggling and wondering why she had taken such a leap by coming to college, was paying off. The moments where she felt disconnected, like an old woman in a sea of youth, faded away. Now, more than her intelligence made her part of this community of learning. She was one of these young dreamers, hurrying off to class. She belonged, in more ways than one. Just like them, she was trying to chase her desires, to become what she had always longed for. Her path was laid out, and it was one she couldn't wait to start down.

She could get her degree in Horticulture, and then get a job at a nursery—maybe manage one. Who knew? Maybe one day, she would own a nursery of her own! Excitement rippled through her, as she held her books to her chest, and took a deep breath.

Genevieve looked at her watch, and realized she was late for her next class. She started running that direction, pausing to do a little skip. Her life would make a difference; she would make her mark on the world! Sure, there was Becca and Joe, but one day Becca would leave, and Joe would always still be his own person. Now, Genevieve could be her own too. Instead of just watching them making their way in the world, Genevieve could join them, making their way together.

She made it to class a couple minutes late, and grabbed the closest seat to the door. The professor looked over at her from the podium, his eyes amused.

"Nice of you to join us, Mrs. Howard. We are discussing Homer's *Odysseus*, and its relevance to modern day movies. Have any input?"

"Um, no...not yet," Genevieve said, heat creeping up her face.

She liked to be able to pretend to be invisible in large groups, and now everyone was starting at her. She could feel the tips of her ears getting hot, as she diverted her attention to her book on the desk. The professor turned, directing his attention to another student. Genevieve felt her heart beat slow, as the pressure was off her.

"Did he say Mrs.?" whispered a voice from behind her.

Genevieve turned to see a girl, who didn't look older than sixteen, peering back at her inquisitively. Genevieve nodded. Other than answering questions or discussions in class, no one usually spoke to Genevieve. The girl tilted her head, sizing Genevieve up.

"Wow, how old are you?" the girl asked, a little too loudly.

Some of the other students around them turned their heads to hear the answer. Genevieve felt her heart speeding up again, and bit her lower lip.

"I'm thirty," Genevieve said, as softly as she could. Many eyebrows raised around her in disbelief.

"No way! I thought you were, like, my age!" the girl gasped, glancing around at the other students, who moved their heads up and down in agreement.

The professor cleared his throat to get their attention, and their eyes snapped back to where he was standing. Genevieve turned to face front and smiled.

A lifetime ago I was, she thought. *Who am I now?*

The house was quiet when she arrived home. Joe should have been home by then, and Becca was out of school hours ago. Worried, she ran up to the house and threw open the door. As she rushed into the living room, she saw Joe sleeping in his easy chair, with Becca curled up beside him. Genevieve let out the breath she hadn't been aware she was holding.

Joe opened one eye wearily, and waved at her. She smiled back at him, laying her books down on the coffee table. They both looked at Becca, and then back at each other. Their eyes met with unspoken understanding. Genevieve tiptoed over and knelt beside the chair. Joe put his arm around her, as Becca stirred slightly and then settled again.

"How was your day at school, darling?"

"It was good, Joe. I made a decision," she replied, resting her head on the arm of the chair.

Joe stroked her head with one hand. Genevieve closed her eyes, soothed by his touch.

"Well, don't keep me in suspense," Joe said finally.

The image of the boy who had said the same thing, outside the cafeteria, popped into her head, making her giggle. She turned her head up, and rested her chin in her hand. Joe watched her with interest. He looked so handsome sitting there, with their baby girl tucked in by his side. He raised his eyebrows, waiting for her answer. That's right, her major.

"Horticulture! You know, plants and things," she said, bobbing her head with excitement.

"I may be old, darling, but I do know what Horticulture is. That's great, you always did have a green thumb," Joe said, and pinched her thumb.

Genevieve slapped at his hand. The sound stirred Becca, who opened her eyes. For a brief moment she appeared a world away, like she had to come back down to put her feet on the ground. Her eyes scanned around, focusing in on Genevieve sitting beside the chair.

"Mommy, we learned about seeds today in school," Becca said, yawning. "Did you know they aren't just for eating?"

"As a matter of fact, sweet potato, I did know that, but tell me more," Genevieve replied, helping Becca off her Daddy's lap.

Becca adjusted the hem of her dress, and rubbed her eyes.

"Oh, I have something to show you!" she exclaimed, and ran out of the room.

She came back in, with a piece of paper, with seeds taped to it. Under each seed, in scribbled writing, was the name of the plant it grew into. Genevieve delicately ran her fingers over the smooth cool seeds, a little thrill running through her. Was this a sign, she had made the right decision? Intuitively, she knew it was.

Gazing at Becca, she thought, *I always have been good at growing things.*

"This is wonderful, Becca, I'm so proud of you!" Genevieve said to her daughter's beaming face.

Becca jumped up and down, and squealed.

Genevieve handed the paper back to Becca. "Can you hang this on the refrigerator, so I can see it every day?"

"Sure, Mommy, I knew you would love it," Becca replied, proud.

Genevieve smiled, as she watched her most prized treasure skipping to the kitchen.

Later that night, as she lay in bed, after tucking in her baby girl to bed, and making love with her husband of eight years, she felt content. She had everything she ever dreamed of, nothing could change that. She knew she was right where she was supposed to be. Nothing could ever cause a ripple in the perfect life they had created for themselves.

Nothing.

Chapter Four

"**My** final year!" Genevieve exclaimed, and thumped her books down at her desk.

Professor Michaels glanced up, smiling. Her blond hair was pulled tightly into a bun, her diamond stud earrings sparkling in the light. She looked like she was ready for a night at the opera, not a day teaching about plants and soil. She adjusted her gold rimmed spectacles, peering at Genevieve with her soft brown eyes.

"Genevieve, you have worked hard. It will be neat to see you mentor some of the newer students this year."

"And, it only took me four...um...plus years to get here!" Genevieve laughed, curtseying rapidly.

"Five and a half years, on a four year degree, is pretty

damn good, actually. I see some people while away their adulthoods in these halls. It's like daycare, for adults with no purpose."

"Prof...I mean Maureen, I really appreciate the extra lab time you've given me. It has helped me keep going. I just do better hands on," Genevieve said, waving her hands in the air for effect.

She and Maureen had become good friends over the last two years, even though, at first, Genevieve found it odd that her professor was a year younger than her. They were complete opposites in how they dressed, spoke, and desired to spend their days, but their love of learning and sense of humor connected them on a totally different level. What always boggled Genevieve's mind, is why Maureen got into teaching sciences, which dealt with the environment. Maureen couldn't stand to get her hands dirty, in the least.

"Ah, the plants in the greenhouse would have all died, if left up to me. My skills are in the books, yours are in your hands," Maureen said, smoothing her hair with a perfectly manicured hand.

Other students filtered in, as Genevieve took her seat by the back of the room. She still felt uncomfortable in large groups, and preferred to hide behind the scenes. At least after this year, she could just work with the plants and be less around people. She felt a kinship when she was tending them, and often found herself singing, or talking, to them. Although she was excited about sharing her own knowledge through the mentor program, the idea of working side by side with another student in the greenhouse less than inspired her.

"Welcome class; please settle so we can get started. This is advanced *Man and His Environment*, the study of human effects on living things in our environment. If you are here by accident, now would be the time to leave. No harm

31

done," Maureen announced to the class.

As in every year, two or three students got up and walked sheepishly out. One even turned and took a bow as he was leaving. A few students applauded, a titter running through the rows, and then the class was quiet again. Maureen adjusted her glasses, clearing her throat, commanding attention just with her mannerisms.

"Every year, we like to have our final year students mentor some of our underclassmen. Today, one of our mentors is with us. Please come up to the front, Genevieve." Maureen motioned back to where Genevieve was sitting.

Before Genevieve could shake her head no, the whole class had turned to look at her. Maureen shrugged unapologetically, as Genevieve glared her direction. Genevieve moved to the front of the class, her face beet red.

Genevieve tried to keep from focusing on any one student with her eyes, waiting until she could go and hide in the back again. She fidgeted with her fingernails, which were constantly embedded with dirt now. Maureen tapped her foot and continued, seemingly oblivious to Genevieve's discomfort.

"Genevieve is a real natural, when it comes to the care of plants. You could find no better person, if you need help in this area. I will assign some of you I feel need extra help to a mentor, but if others would like one, please let me know after class. The slots fill up quickly, so don't dawdle if you think you would like to be part of this program. Your mentor will be grading you—this is not a slacker's course. Only sign up if you are serious. Okay, Genevieve, you can be seated."

Genevieve made sure to throw back an *'I'm going to get you'* glance to Maureen, and slipped back to her seat.

Maureen pretended not to notice, and got right into her lecture. Maureen was not one to waste time, when it came to learning. A few students looked around at each other; they knew they were in for it this year in Professor Michaels' class. Genevieve chuckled, remembering how she had felt just the opposite. It was a lot easier to focus on the materials for her, than on socialization.

The rest of the period went by without incident, much to Genevieve's relief. As soon as it was over, she rushed out to the greenhouse to tend the plants. Once inside she inhaled deeply, the aromas of fresh soil, flowers, and greenery filling her head. She exhaled, letting all the stress of the day melt away.

Checking off a mental duty list, she walked around to all the pots, some with tiny sprouts poking through, others still dormant, waiting for life to began, and yet others in full bloom. Finally, she checked all the automatic sprinklers to make sure they were on. A fine spray of mist started, and the cool water felt delicious on her skin. She leaned in and sniffed the marigolds in bloom, and thought about how her hands, in many ways, gave them life. Their life, in turn, gave hers meaning. In here, she felt in tune with life and her purpose in it. People flustered her, while plants calmed her.

After all the plants were taken care of, Genevieve sat down on the floor, and opened her brown paper lunch sack. She rested against a stack of crates, and started to eat a roasted-pepper and marble-jack cheese on rye sandwich. Joe thought her sandwich concoctions were disgusting, but she liked them anyway. He was a meat and potatoes guy, swearing she was an old hippie at heart. She pulled out a bottle of water, took a sip, and closed her eyes, relaxing in the solitude of the greenhouse.

In many ways, she couldn't believe she was going to

graduate at the end of the year, and leave this place for good. It had become as much part of her life, as her own home was. The idea of having to walk out those doors at the end of the year, didn't sit well with her.

The years of school had taken its toll on her family. Especially Joe and her. They still talked and laughed, but the passion had faded. Joe worked long hours at the construction site, when he came home he was usually exhausted. They still sat and watched television, and talked about Becca, politics, the world, and all the other things they had always shared.

It was the part of them, which made her catch her breath that was gone—chased away by their busy schedules, maybe Joe's age, or perhaps just familiarity. Whatever it was, Genevieve longed greatly to feel the stirring, which had once made it hard for them to keep their hands off each other.

Becca was eleven now, and didn't seem to need her parents so much anymore. She was a bright child, and very beautiful. The boys were already starting to call, which made Joe mad. He still saw Becca as his little girl. Genevieve often felt like she was running interference between Becca and Joe, and she missed the days when Becca was simply Daddy's girl.

All that was different now, most times Genevieve felt alone at home. She found she looked forward to heading out each morning for school, lingering longer than needed at the greenhouse in the evenings. During the summer, she stayed as busy as she could landscaping their yard, which had turned from a dusty weedy plot into a gorgeous green lawn, lined with flowers of all colors and sizes. People often slowed as they drove by, just to take in the beauty she had created.

Her thoughts were interrupted by the sound of

Maureen's voice, coming into the greenhouse. Maureen almost never came down to the greenhouse, making Genevieve wonder what on earth Maureen was doing so far from the clean walls of the main building. She quickly ate the last bite of her sandwich, washing it down with the last of her bottled water. She was still sitting on the floor, behind the middle row of counters, packing up her stuff, when the door of the greenhouse swung open. Maureen was talking to someone excitedly about the mentor program. It was her baby, after all.

"Now, I think the best person to have you mentor with is Genevieve. Even though you aren't a Horticulture Major, your studies in the environmental studies are perfectly matched. Since you are studying to be a Naturalist, the best way to get in touch with local flora is to work in the greenhouse, hands on."

"I appreciate you letting me come into the program this year, Professor Michaels. It really will help me to learn by doing, rather than just through books and pictures," a low male voice answered.

Genevieve realized she hadn't been noticed, and didn't know if she should make her presence known after sitting there so long. Maybe they would leave in a minute or two, once they saw she wasn't there, and she could stand up then. A metal post was poking in her leg uncomfortably, even though she tried to shift to a more comfortable position. She hoped they would head out soon. Instead they kept talking.

"Not a problem, this is a fairly new program, and we are excited to see such interest in it. I was hoping Genevieve would be here to introduce you to. Gosh, usually she runs right over here after class. I can't imagine where she is off to."

"Professor, may I stay and look around for awhile… in

case she comes back?" the voice asked.

Say no, say no! Genevieve shrieked in her mind.

"Sure thing, stay as long as you would like. Just sign out when you leave. If Genevieve shows up, let her know I have paired you with her this year, for the mentor program. Genevieve is a funny one. She's… well… you'll see," Maureen said, and chuckled.

What's that remark supposed to mean? Genevieve thought. *I'm what?*

She heard Maureen's heels clacking out, and then the door bang shut.

Now what? She thought. *Here I was eavesdropping, and now he's going to find me.*

Mustering all the courage she could, she stood up and cleared her throat. A young man was standing with his back to her, leaning over pots of tickseed. His broad shoulders tightened with surprise, at the realization that he was not alone. When he turned around, she found herself staring into the most gorgeous blue eyes she had ever seen. She was suddenly aware that her breath must smell like roasted peppers, and took a small step back.

"Uh… hello, I'm Genevieve. I promise I'm not a stalker, I'm your mentor," she sputtered, sticking her hand awkwardly out.

He laughed, and shook it with his own. His hand was warm, but sent a delightful shiver down her spine. He stood a few inches taller than her, his presence making her breath come a little faster. She dropped her hand to her side, shaking off the feeling. The young man shyly ran his hand through his blond, curly hair.

"Hi, I'm Danny."

Chapter Five

Genevieve's heart skipped a beat when he said his name. Standing here looking at this young man, seemed so familiar to her. What was it about him? She rubbed her chin lightly, as she racked her brain trying to figure out what the connection was. All of a sudden, he smiled and it lit up his whole face.

"I don't bite, you know," he said, his blue eyes glittering.

Her breath caught in her throat, when the memories came flooding back. He was the boy, from so many years ago! The shy, thin boy, who had mowed her lawn that day over ten years ago. Genevieve burst out laughing at the changes in him! He was definitely no longer the scrawny child, who had struggled to push the mower through the overgrown weeds in her lawn. Standing before her, was a full grown man, who had lost all skinniness, and replaced it with muscles and height.

"Oh my! You have grown up so much. *You're* the little Danny, who mowed my lawn?"

"One and the same. You haven't changed a bit," he replied, his whole skin turning a light shade of pink.

Genevieve sincerely doubted it, but was flattered by his comment, nonetheless. They stood there staring at each other, both too shy to move. Finally, Genevieve, in a grand attempt to make a smooth getaway, stepped backwards, and fell over the crates she had been leaning against! Well, almost fell. She braced herself to hit the floor, hoping she would miss the metal spike, which had been poking her earlier. Instead, she felt a strong arm grab her firmly. In a second, she was upright again, and she found herself standing not a hair's breath away from Danny, his hand still gripping her arm. The heat that radiated off his body, made her feel lightheaded.

"Thanks, I mean, thank you... I'm alright," she stammered.

He gently let go of her arm, she stepped away trembling. His eyes never left her face, and she looked quickly to the floor.

"How's this, for an awkward first meeting?" Genevieve asked, blushing.

"Second, actually," he said, and laughed.

Genevieve knew she had to break the tension, so she grabbed a broom, and shoved it into his hands.

"Okay, since I will be your mentor this year, our first order of business is to clean up the greenhouse. It has been totally neglected this past summer. You start sweeping over there. I'll start labeling all the plants, and organizing the seed cabinet. That is, if you want to get started today?"

He nodded and took the broom, sauntering over to the other side of the greenhouse. He started sweeping vigorously, making quick work of the floor. Genevieve caught herself staring at the smooth movement of his back muscles, with each sweep. *Get it together girl,* she thought, and snatched up a package of labels. She turned her back to get to work.

They worked in silence for over an hour. When they were done, the greenhouse practically sparkled. The sun was starting to go down, and Genevieve's stomach grumbled from hunger. She pressed down on it, trying to silence the rumbling, hoping Danny hadn't heard its noisy complaint. She glanced rapidly over at him. If he had heard, he pretended not to notice. He was peering down at the labels of the plants, as he touched each one to match its name. Genevieve admired the way his fingers delicately brushed over each leaf, without disturbing them.

"I'm majoring in Horticulture. I love being in here with all the plants," Genevieve said quietly.

Danny glanced up at her, and smiled. "I'm majoring in Environmental Sciences."

"How did you end up in the Horticulture mentor program, then?" Genevieve asked, confused.

"I asked Professor Michaels if I could be considered, because I wanted to have a more hands-on experience—to learn all the different plants. I figure I have to know what I want to preserve. That was at least one of the reasons," he said cryptically.

"Oh, that makes perfect sense. Well, tomorrow we can start going through some of the different plants. I basically have them all memorized, but I won't expect you to know all of them. It's just good to have a feel for the plants, and their care."

"I'm looking forward to it," Danny said, peeking over at Genevieve.

Their eyes locked for a second, and Genevieve grinned. There was just something about Danny that made her feel calm. Most people in this close of proximity made her nervous, babbling uncontrollably. Danny seemed to like silence as much as she did, and she was relieved she had been paired with him for the mentor program.

Danny picked up the broom, moving past her to the closet. He opened the door, and hung it on the hook. As his arm was up, Genevieve noticed a large scar running down the back of his arm. She resisted the urge to reach out and trace it with her fingers. She wondered how he got such a large scar, which ran from his shoulder almost to his elbow, and winced.

She knew she hadn't seen it when he was a boy mowing her lawn, otherwise she would have questioned him then. He turned, and saw where her eyes were focused. He cleared his throat softly. Genevieve snapped her eyes up embarrassed, meeting his gaze. He shrugged and smiled. She tried to smile back, but her lips just wobbled. She quickly looked down, and fiddled with the leaves of one of the plants. She felt him come over, and stand next to her.

"It's alright," he said softly. "It happened when I was a kid. My dad beat the crap out of me, one day."

"For what?" Genevieve asked, aghast at what would lead a father to do such a horrible act.

"I took something of his without asking."

"What on earth could you have taken, that would make him so mad?" Genevieve asked, her eyes wide with disbelief.

"His lawn mower. I borrowed it, to mow the lawn of a pretty woman I found myself drawn to... when I was ten," he replied, his voice shaking slightly. "It was stupid of me to do, especially in my house."

Genevieve stared at him, fear gripping her chest, with the comprehension of whose lawn he was talking about. He watched her, not even blinking. He had gotten beaten for mowing her lawn! He wasn't out just making extra money; he had come to see her! That's how he had known her name back then. What she thought was a random meeting, was actually a small boy reaching out to a woman he felt a connection to. She had sent him on his way that day, having no idea the hell he was about to endure.

"I'm so sorry," Genevieve whispered. She couldn't help but reach out, and touch the scar. Her fingers ran down the length of it, and she felt his muscles tighten underneath. "What did he use that caused this?"

"A garden claw. He kept yelling if I wanted to play in other people's gardens, I would need the right tools."

Genevieve felt sick, picturing what must have happened. She was the kind of parent who didn't even spank, and in her heart she just couldn't understand a parent who would draw blood on their own child. How did he ever come out of that okay? A tear escaped and slipped down Genevieve's cheek, into the plant she was standing above. She felt his fingers reach out and wipe her cheek. She wiped her eyes, embarrassed to cry in front of someone she hardly knew. Then again, the crossing of their paths had made a huge impact on his life as a child.

"It's okay, you didn't cause this. It wasn't the first time he beat me. It was the last, because the State came and took me away. Things got a lot better after that. In some ways, it was the price I paid to gain my freedom," Danny said gently.

Genevieve couldn't fathom a father being so cruel. Joe was always so loving with Becca, even when Becca was being horrid. Even though she and Joe were more just friends anymore, she was grateful he was such a wonderful dad to their little girl. That reason alone, had kept her love for him burning strong.

"Did you find me again by accident?" Genevieve asked, curious if this was just another chance encounter.

"More or less. I was taking courses here the past two years. This year, I saw you listed as a mentor for a program I was interested in anyhow."

"So, you asked Professor Michaels if I could be your mentor?"

"Yeah, but she thought we were a good match anyway. I promise I'm not a stalker, just your mentored," he said, and chuckled.

Genevieve sniffed and wiped her nose. She didn't know how she felt about all the revelations of the day, but her heart told her this was just the beginning. For some reason, that little boy had come back into her life, and it had to be more than coincidence. As if he was reading her mind, Danny stared at the floor, and scuffed his shoe against the planks.

"Genevieve, I don't think it was an accident we met again. I think it's fate."

Chapter Six

Every school day, after their final classes, Danny and Genevieve met up at the greenhouse for the mentor program. They worked in silence at first, skirting around each other at a distance. Each day would be the same—the glances, clearing of throats, and uncomfortable periods of deafening silence. It got to the point where Genevieve brought in a CD player, to drown out the nothingness. Before long, they found themselves working to the music, even keeping up with the rhythms. Soon the tension faded, and one or the other started small talk. In a matter of time, they were laughing and joking around.

"Hey, Gen, can you hand me the stack of labels over there?"

"What, are your legs broken? Get them yourself, gimpy!"

"Suit yourself," Danny said, dragging his right leg behind him dramatically.

Genevieve laughed, and swatted at him with her glove. He grabbed it mid-air, and swatted her on the behind with it. Genevieve feigned disgust.

"Oh, you dirty dog!" she shrieked at him. She snatched the glove back, sticking her face up in the air. As he brushed past her, she could feel the electricity between their bodies.

Get a grip, Genevieve, he's just a baby. A baby in a man's body.

She tried to focus on the seeds she was planting, but her eyes just kept sliding over to look at him. How could he be the same little boy, now leaning over with those long, sinewy arms? Her mind knew she needed to see him strictly as her student and as a friend, but her body kept taking turns down the wrong path. Almost like having a crush on a celebrity, except this crush was around her everyday, within arm's reach. She shook her head, and walked to the other side of the greenhouse. It would be easier to focus on the task at hand, as far away as possible.

"What? Do I smell?" Danny asked, after Genevieve had pressed herself against the far wall, bowing her head to study the seeds lists.

She bit her lip, as she peered over at him. "No, Danny, it's just that…," she stopped.

Exactly, how would one say they were attracted to someone almost young enough to be their son? Okay, maybe not quite, but close enough. And she was married! Yet, Danny made her heart race, and her feel things she knew she shouldn't. Danny stopped what he was doing and watched her. His eyes locked onto hers. His head bobbed slightly in understanding.

"I know," he said simply.

Her heart started to race. *Snap out of it!* She let her eyes drop, but still felt his eyes on her. Her fingers toyed with the metal label rods on the counter, as she tried to think of a way to change the subject.

She bent down to pull out some more pots from underneath the counter, keeping her back to Danny for some time. When she stood back up, he was standing over the front counter, with the plant index book opened in front of him. His eyes were closed, and he was reciting the names of the plants alphabetically.

She watched him for awhile, liking the way that when he forgot what came next, he would make circles with his hands. She couldn't help herself, and laughed out loud. Danny opened his eyes, raising his eyebrows as he looked over at her.

"I'm sorry, it's just that you look like a conductor, leading the plants in a symphony," Genevieve snorted.

Danny looked slightly offended, and then laughed an infectious baritone sound. "Ah, music was always my first love. I even have a cat named Sousa."

"After the composer?"

"Yup."

"Wow, you have a cat? You don't seem like a cat person," Genevieve said, wrinkling up her nose. She had never known a man to actually *like* cats.

Danny tilted his head at her, and frowned. "I didn't know a cat person had a look. I mean, no, I don't wear three different sweaters at the same time, and carry around toy mice in my pocket. He's cool though, keeps me company."

"Oh, I didn't mean to offend you! I like cats too... dogs mostly, but cats too. So, you don't live in the dorms then?"

Genevieve asked, feeling like she was on a fishing expedition.

"Nope, too much noise. I like it quiet. I have an apartment about two miles from here. Just me and Sousa." Danny seemed to accentuate the fact it was just him and The March King.

At the word 'apartment', Genevieve's mind started to wander down the wrong path again. She thought about what his apartment would look like. A typical bachelor pad, or a neat place with modern art on the walls? Did he cook, or eat take out? Did he make his bed everyday? His bed. A single...or a double? White cotton sheets, or something more exotic?

Her mind wandered into further forbidden territory. She wondered if he was a gentle lover, would he caress her slowly and look into her eyes? Would he hold her tenderly, and stroke her face? She imagined pressing her bare body against his, as he whispered into her ear. Her fingers running through his curly hair, his hand pressed at the back of her nape...

"Genevieve!"

She snapped back into reality, to hear him calling her name. She flushed from head to toe, her eyes wide with surprise. As she whirled to meet his gaze, she found herself speechless. She cleared her throat, which felt tight and dry. What would he think; if he had known she was mentally undressing him, and more, right then and there?

"What's going on? You blanked out there for a minute. Are you okay?" he asked, concerned.

Genevieve smiled a little too wide at him, her teeth feeling wooden. "I'm... more than okay, just got distracted."

"By what?"

"By, well... " She laughed nervously, "Um... just

something I have to do."

Brilliant, Genevieve.

He nodded his head and smirked. Did he know? He couldn't possibly, but the electricity still hung in the air. She thought if she reached out and touched his arm at that moment; a spark would shoot between them.

"Well, looks like we are done for the day. Want to grab a bite to eat?" Danny asked, looking around to make sure the greenhouse was in proper order.

The misters kicked on, and filled the space with a cool wetness. Genevieve rubbed her arms, the moisture disappearing quickly into her skin.

"No, I'd better get home. I have a hormonal preteen and an over-protective father, to keep separated. Thanks for the offer though, maybe we could do lunch on campus one day."

"Ah, family. That's right. Well, I'll see you tomorrow then, Gen."

No one had ever called her Gen before, but she liked when Danny did. It was almost as if when she was here with him, it was just them in the world. Ever since Joe, she hadn't felt so close to another man. Nowadays, she spent more time with Danny than Joe. She reminded herself that she had a family, a marriage to focus on.

Enough fantasizing about younger men, girl.

Danny collected up his books, and touched his eyebrow with two fingers in a wave, before he headed out. Genevieve locked up the greenhouse and strolled down the path to the parking lot. It was getting late. Most likely, Joe would be eating peanut butter and jelly sandwiches, if she didn't hurry home soon. That, or he and Becca would be in a yelling match before long.

Genevieve knew that Becca had a boy at school she considered her "boyfriend", and Joe would flip if he found out. She didn't like lying to Joe, but sometimes she felt he was just too old-fashioned, for this day and age. After all, Becca, and this boy did little more than passing notes, and stare at each other in the hallways at school. At their age, that constituted a relationship, Genevieve chuckled to herself. Back when life was so simple.

Sometimes, Genevieve missed those days. Maybe that's what she was seeing in Danny. A chance to be a starry-eyed school girl, newly in infatuation. She knew it was stupid; she needed to let it go. She climbed behind the wheel, and started up the car.

As she pulled out of the parking lot, heading for home, she told herself it was time to just grow up. So many women her age were already divorced, for at least the first time, and there were those like Maureen, who had never found the love of her life. She was one in a hundred, to have such a perfect supportive husband waiting for her at home.

The car tooled quietly down Main Street. The sunset cast a pinkish-purple light on the buildings around her, making everything look like a flavor of cotton candy. College kids stood outside the theatre playing hacky-sack, joking around with each other.

Their night was just starting, while Genevieve's was wrapping up. A tinge of jealously shot through her, and she turned her eyes back towards the road. It had been her choice to put off college, and get married young. Becca had come along quickly, but they hadn't made any real attempts to prevent parenthood.

At twenty-three, Genevieve thought all she would ever want would be within the four walls of their house. For awhile it was. Then college filled another void. Deep within her a voice cried out that she was still pushing part of her away, so she didn't have to face up to it.

"Don't be ridiculous, Genevieve," she whispered to herself, turning the radio up, as if to drown out the voice in her soul.

Yet, as the sun dropped behind the horizon, a sadness came over her that she just couldn't shake.

Chapter Seven

"**Mooomm**! I can't find my pink shoes!"

"Becca, hold your horses, I'm coming," Genevieve shouted up the stairs, exasperated.

There was nothing like a preteen going to her first dance. Becca was celebrating her twelfth birthday, with a teeny-bopper dance and pizza. Genevieve spotted the pink shoes by the bottom of the stairs, and picked them up, shaking her head in disbelief. Becca was almost in the same shoes size as her. Where did her baby girl go? She headed up the stairs, two at a time, just as Becca started to call her again.

Becca was standing by her bed, staring at two dresses laid out. Sheer panic gripped her face, as she looked back and forth between the two equally beautiful, gowns. As Genevieve came in, she clasped her hands together frantically.

"Mom, which dress should I wear? I look stupid in both!"

Nothing could be further from the truth. Becca had managed to get the best traits of each of her parents, and was already starting to develop into a gorgeous young woman. This little fact had not escaped Joe's notice. He had gone into hyper-drive as Protector Dad. Genevieve reflected on her own developing years, wishing Becca just knew how lucky she was to have a dad, who even took the time to notice her. Genevieve didn't know whether to laugh or cry, watching her daughter go through puberty. It was like a tornado most days, with a lot of torrential downpours.

"I don't know, sweetie, both are beautiful," Genevieve said, stroking her daughter's long brown hair. "Show them both to me on, maybe I can help you choose."

Becca nodded, grabbed the dresses, and headed for the bathroom. That was another new factor in their lives. Becca craved privacy at all times. Except, when she decided she would allow Joe and Genevieve in for a brief glimpse into her life. Genevieve sighed, and sat back on Becca's bed.

She envied Becca, in so many ways. At Becca's age, Genevieve had spent more time with her grandma than her own parents. They had very little time for their only child, and shuttled her off as much as they could. Her parents were both born and raised in Chadron, but seemed to detest living there. Her mother didn't need to work, because her father made a substantial income as a traveling doctor between the many rural towns in the area. In their free time they traveled to the larger cities for "culture", as they called it, but Genevieve now thought they were missing out on the real culture of Chadron. They definitely missed out on their daughter's life.

Becca peeked her head out the door, and then emerged in a picture of pink satin and tulle. It caught Genevieve's breath, seeing her young daughter dressed like a princess. Becca had always been more of a tomboy, and had previously worn dresses only under duress. She clapped her hands, and Becca grinned. She twirled, putting her arms in the air.

"What do you think, Mom?" she asked coyly, as if she didn't know.

"Oh, Bec, you are so beautiful," Genevieve answered, with tears in her eyes. "My baby has grown up too fast."

Becca rolled her eyes and groaned. She slipped back into the bathroom in a flash. A few minutes later, she stepped out, this time in a tight-fitting, white, lace dress, with pink flowers on the hem. This one showed off her newly blooming figure, more than Genevieve knew Joe would allow. She waved her hands back towards the bathroom, shaking her head no. Becca slumped her shoulders and disappeared back inside. The decision was made by default.

While she was waiting for her daughter to come back out, for final preparations, Genevieve lay back on the bed, and thought about her own teen years. She had been alone most of the time, and with her grandma the remaining time. When she started her period, she was alone, too mortified to tell anyone. She went to the neighbors, claiming to be locked out. She raided the woman's bathroom for supplies, while the woman called Genevieve's grandma to come and let her in. After Grandma arrived, and they were back in the safety of Grandma's living room, Genevieve let the truth spill out. Grandma had held her hand, and rubbed her head, soothing away her fears. They had sat up drinking coffee late into the night, as Grandma had filled in all Genevieve's questions.

Her father passed away her senior year in high school, but she hardly missed him. The town had done a lot of pomp and circumstance, about how they just didn't know how they would go on without his medical, and people, skills. Genevieve had just felt empty, and saw very little change in her day to day life. Her mother died the year Becca was born, but she had been remarried, and moved across the country by then. Genevieve didn't even attend the funeral.

When Joe asked if she was alright, she simply said, "About what?"

Her parents had never been outwardly unkind, but they had never included Genevieve in their lives. If it hadn't been for her grandma, Genevieve would have felt totally alone most of her young life.

She hoped Becca would have a better relationship with her and Joe, over time. She knew a gap had grown when she had gone back to college, but she only had three months left before she graduated. She planned to open her own nursery after graduation. They had been saving money, so she could start it up. There was a lot near the construction equipment yard Joe owned he had offered to let her use. It seemed like the perfect solution.

She heard the bathroom door creak, and sat back up to see Becca come back into the room in a whoosh of pink satin. Becca sat down quietly next to her mother, and laid her head on Genevieve's shoulder. Genevieve was both startled and touched by this gesture. Becca had spent so much time pushing her away the last couple of years, Genevieve didn't know what brought this on. She put her arm around Becca's thin shoulders, and for just a moment

Becca was her baby girl again. Genevieve reveled in the quiet moment, wishing she could have a picture of these ever fleeting instances.

Too soon, Becca shrugged off her mother's arm, and stood up. She grabbed the hairbrush off the nightstand, and started yanking away at her hair. Genevieve gently took the brush, and began to work on Becca's hair, which reached down past her shoulder blades. The hair felt like fine silk in Genevieve's hand, she admired its smooth flowing texture, compared to her own wavy crazy hair. Although Joe had always had a touch of gray in his hair, Genevieve imagined that the same smooth chestnut hair that adorned Becca's head, must have been what his was in his earlier years. A soft sigh escaped from Becca's lips, as her shoulders slumped forward.

"Baby, you know how much Daddy and I love you, right?"

"Yeah, I know, Mom. Dad just gives me such a hard time about everything, all the time."

"Becca, he just wants to keep you safe, and daddies all too often try to keep their little girls safe by over-protecting them, and blowing a lot of smoke."

"I am not a little girl anymore," Becca said, annunciating each word.

Genevieve held back the laugh, which threatened to escape her chest. That would not bode well with her fragile daughter right now.

"But to us, you will always be our little girl, even when you're sixty, and I'm eighty-three," Genevieve replied. She could tell that as much as Becca was irritated by that fact, she also appreciated she had parents she could take for granted.

"There now, don't you look lovely," Genevieve said, as she applied a light coat of lip gloss to Becca's lips.

Becca genuinely smiled, then slipped on her matching satin shoes. When she stood up and faced Genevieve, her mother's heart swelled with love. Who was this willowy creature, standing before her? She reached out and hugged Becca, kissing her on the cheek.

They came down the stairs together to show Joe Becca's dress. As they came around the corner, he stood up, and even Genevieve could see the tears in his eyes. He cleared his throat, as he shifted from one foot to the other. She was still their little girl, but in this moment, they both were aware the years until she was a woman were fast approaching. Joe came over, and took Becca's hand. He gently twirled her around. His eyes met Genevieve's, and they both smiled.

"Now, no slow dances—and you have to stay a foot apart. No touching!" Joe said, half-seriously.

"Oh, Dad," Becca moaned.

Joe reached out, pinching her cheek lightly. They looked at each other, and then laughed. With all the battles and tension between them lately, somewhere deep down Becca really wanted to be his little girl, and Joe really wanted her to shine.

Genevieve grabbed the camera and started snapping pictures, just as a horn honked signaling Becca's ride. Becca made an impatient face at Genevieve, who continued to pose her for the ideal photo shots. Becca inched towards the door, gripping the handle. Genevieve chuckled and nodded, to set her free from the photo session. Becca grinned and flew out the door.

After Becca had left with her friends for the dance, Genevieve sat down next to Joe on the couch, clicking on the television with the remote. There was just something so comfortable about being with him, as if neither had to wonder what the other wanted, or was thinking. She leaned against his shoulder, and closed her eyes, worn out from the preparations of Becca's big night. Joe yawned, and took her hand in his own. Joe wasn't getting any younger, and she realized he wasn't so different in age than her own father was when he passed away. Joe was forty-eight, and all the years of hard working were taking their toll on his body.

Genevieve's age was showing less, and Joe's was showing more. She wondered if it was a man-woman thing, or just the way things were. Perhaps it was all the years in construction, which were less than kind to a body.

People often mistook her for Becca's sister, while they thought Joe was Becca's grandfather. They laughed it off, but she wondered if it ever secretly bothered him. She loved him though, and none of that really mattered. There were times she wished they made love more, that he still made her heart race, but she knew that she had a good marriage. That needed to be preserved. She supposed all marriages went through this after ten, or so, years.

She lifted her head up, and saw Joe had fallen asleep. She nudged him to see if he would wake up. He didn't budge, and she knew he would want to stay downstairs, to be there when Becca came home. She sighed and squeezed his hand, before she got up to shut things down for the night. As Genevieve climbed the stairs, she glanced back at her sleeping husband, and questioned if she was destined to spend the rest of her life being in bed alone. Even when he was lying next to her, she felt like she was on an island of longing by herself.

Chapter Eight

Danny was sitting down peering at seeds through a microscope, when Genevieve came into the greenhouse. During the past six months, he had absorbed everything she had to show him like a sponge. He had become extremely interested in how seeds and plants adapt and mutate to live, when outside factors, namely man, changed things around them. He raised his hand and waved, without ever looking up, when he heard her come in. Genevieve smiled softly in his direction, marveling at how close of friends they had become since he joined the mentor program.

Genevieve set down her back-pack on the counter, and picked up her list for the day. She gazed around the greenhouse, which was thriving. In the next few months, some of their study plants, which had bloomed, would be taken over to Porter James Nursing Home to be planted. The college did that every year, under Genevieve's guidance.

Her own grandma had spent the last of her years in Porter James, and Genevieve remembered how much the little things had meant to her. The residents loved to see the flowers out their windows, and often asked to be escorted to the gardens just to sit. Many of them talked of their own gardens they had cultivated, before coming to the nursing home. Genevieve heard the sadness in their voices. This was something she could do to make their days a little brighter.

Genevieve brought in a proposal to the college the second year she had attended, about taking the annual flowers over to the nursing home, after the college was done with them. Since annuals have to be replanted every year, and a large portion of seeds were kept from the plants, she couldn't see the harm in sharing the flowers.

The college had readily agreed, as long as Genevieve headed up the project, and it took nothing away from the ongoing Horticulture program. The nursing home had always welcomed the college's nursing students in, for hands-on experience, so this was a way for the college to show their appreciation.

She breathed deeply, all the different essences of the flowers filling her nose. She looked around with pride at their accomplishments this year. She knew without Danny, she would not have been able to do so much. Her eyes rested on him, and then on the scar on the back of his arm. How could he be so well adjusted, growing up in the horrible environment of his childhood? How could anyone live through that, and still be such a kind and open person? Maybe, he was like the seeds he was studying.

"Danny, can I ask you something?"

"Sure, what's up?" he replied, with his eye still pressed to the eyepiece.

When she didn't speak right away, he looked up and spun around to see her, his face a mixture of curiosity and humor.

"Well, after you were taken away from your parents... where did you go?" Genevieve asked timidly. She pulled a stool over to face him, and sat down.

He regarded her for a moment, and then stared down at his hands. When he looked back up, she could see storms behind his eyes.

"First I went to the hospital... " They both flinched, when he said this. "Then, since no immediate family was willing to take me, I went to a boy's home. I spent about five months there. A non-blood aunt of mine found out I was in there, so she fought the system to get me out. I guess she was married to my mom's uncle, but he had died. At first, the State didn't even consider to ask her. My Aunt Bridget raised me until I was out on my own. She taught me what a real adult is supposed to be like."

"Danny... I hate to ask this, but did you ever go back to see your parents—after you grew up?"

A bitter look crossed his face, for a moment he looked like the stoic little boy, who had once knocked on her door. Then a flash of anger crossed his face, and he gritted his teeth.

"Why would I? If someone kidnapped you, beat you, tormented you, made you feel like you were worthless, would it make you want to spend time with them—just because they were family?" he asked vehemently.

"I'm sorry. No, of course not. I'm sorry, I shouldn't have asked. It's none of my business. I'm sorry," Genevieve stammered, and stood up flustered. She felt stupid and embarrassed for bringing up such a painful memory for him. Her cheeks burned with humiliation. She wanted to run and hide.

As she started to step away, his arm snaked out and grabbed her wrist. She glimpsed down at him, at the clouds darkening his eyes. He rose and pulled her towards him, wrapping his arms around her. She leaned her forehead against his chest, her arms tightly around his waist, and kept murmuring 'I'm sorry'.

"Shhhh, baby, it's okay. Shhhh," he whispered, until she settled down.

She could hear his heart beating rapidly in his chest, contrary to what his lips were saying. She relaxed, and let her body rest against his. Soon his heart beat slowed, and they both stood there intertwined calmly.

She gazed up into his placid blue eyes. He smiled at her, just like the Danny she had known for all these months. She knew it was okay, that he knew she meant no discontent in her questions. She had simply wanted to know more, about someone she had grown to genuinely care about.

They both let go of each other at the same time, and she stepped back. It wasn't awkward, or uncomfortable. She reached up to his face, touching his cheek softly, her fingers saying what her mouth couldn't. He caught her fingers, and pressed them to his lips. Then he let her hand go.

"Gen, thank you for caring. I'm sorry it got so heated. I just erased that part of my life. I don't think about it... almost ever. There's no good in it."

"Oh, Danny, I should have thought about that. You are just so... so put together. You seem so unaffected by it all," she said. She saw a brief shadow cross his eyes, before his brilliant smile lit of his face again.

"It's all a facade, baby, just a facade."

The rest of the afternoon passed, with each of them working on their own projects. Genevieve was working on her final Thesis for graduation, even though it was still months away, and Danny on his studies of adaptation. She knew in a few months she would be leaving, but he still had another year of school left. Their lives would take separate paths after that, and she knew she would miss their long talks and humorous banter. It made her sad to think she might not see her friend so often.

That's what it is, she thought.

Becca was her daughter, Joe her husband, but Danny was her friend. Someone she shared a lot in common with, without strings attached. Joe was a friend too, but on a different level. Danny was someone who she didn't have to ever fight with, someone who she could just be herself with. A friend who she never had to play devil's advocate with, a friend who saw her simply as a woman, as a student… as Genevieve.

Over the last six months they had worked side by side, laughing, talking, and sharing. Even though they had shared painful memories of their past, and frustrations of their lives, when they left the greenhouse doors neither had to carry each other's burdens. Although, she felt with what had happened today, she was more than willing to carry his burdens—to truly know her friend.

"I had a sister, you know," she heard him say, from across the room.

She looked over, surprised. He had never mentioned a sister, or any siblings. He said *had*, not have. He didn't have her anymore. She had assumed, like her, he was an only child. Danny looked up, with his face sadder than she had ever seen it, his eyes off in a distant memory.

"They say she died of SIDS," he said in a whisper. "But

I know otherwise."

Genevieve walked over to him, slowly, frightened by what she thought she might hear. What had happened? His head was hanging low, his hands pressed against the counter, his arms braced as if to hold him up. Genevieve moved over behind him, and placed a hand on his back. His t-shirt was damp with sweat, and his muscles were rigid. He took a deep breath, going on.

"Her name was Emily; I just called her 'baby'. I was four, when she was born. I would sit by her crib, and look at her in awe. I couldn't wait until she was big enough for me to play with," he stopped, and stood quietly.

Genevieve could almost hear his blood coursing through his veins. He sighed and went on.

"They would let her cry so much. She would just lay there and scream. When they would come to get her, they would yank her up so fast; I thought her head would snap off. Then, they would yell at her to shut up. I would hide under her crib, because if they saw me they would smack me—just because I was there. How she lived through those first few months, I don't know."

"What happened to her?" Genevieve asked, her heart in her throat.

Danny turned around and faced her, lines of distress etching his face.

"When she was eight months old, I would climb in the crib with her, and we would play. That kept her happy most times, but when she was hungry she would cry, and they would get mad again. Sometimes they slapped her. I tried to protect her, but they would push, or kick, me away. One night... " his voice cracked, and his body broke into a sob.

Genevieve could feel him trying to fight it back. She put her hand on his arm for comfort. "Shhh, it's okay," she

62

murmured. "You don't have to tell me."

"No, I do. Someone else has to know this," he said hoarsely. He rubbed his nose hard and continued. "One night I heard her crying, so I went in to check on her. My mother was standing over the crib with a pillow, and she put it over Em's face. I ran up and tried to stop her, but she threw me away. Her eyes looked like the devil's. I ran back up and grabbed her, trying to pull her away from the baby, but I couldn't move her. I screamed at her to please *stop*. She just kept pressing the pillow, and pressing it. Then she left, as if nothing had happened. I climbed into Emily's crib to see if she was okay. She just laid there, her eyes open staring, but I knew she wasn't in there anymore. I called her name, but she just laid there."

Genevieve stepped forward, enfolding Danny in her arms. He spun and held her against him so tightly, like a drowning victim holding on to something for dear life. His voice was barely above a whisper, when he started to speak again.

"I climbed out of the crib and went to bed, hoping Emily would be there in the morning, laughing and playing, like she usually was. I was woken up by my mother screaming in Emily's room. I dashed in, and she was holding Emily's lifeless body, as if she didn't know what she had done, but I knew she did. The police and an ambulance came later, and took Emily's body away. They kept consoling my mother, like she was somehow a grieving parent. I should have said something, but I was so afraid she would come and put a pillow over my face too. So I never did." His body started to shake hard, with years of pent up silence.

Genevieve held him as tight as she could. For a moment he held on to her, and then suddenly he jerked and pushed her away. She could see the torment in his face, as he moved away from her. He backed towards the doors of the greenhouse. Genevieve reached out to stop him, but he put his hand up to keep her away. He threw the door open and stumbled out into the night. She chased after him.

"Danny, wait! Don't go!" she cried, but he started to run—disappearing into dark.

She went back inside, her mind trying to make sense of what she had just heard. She sat on the floor, and put her head in her hands. She couldn't believe the things he had said. It was no wonder he never spoke to his parents again. Her mind drifted back to the day he had mowed her lawn. She wished she had known the horror he had lived through then, so she could have rescued him. That little boy who knocked on her door had been crying out for help, and he was still knocking.

Chapter Nine

The next day, Danny did not show up to the greenhouse. Genevieve figured he just needed some time alone. She couldn't imagine what it was like for him, to tell someone the secret he had been holding in for so many years. Besides, they were good friends; she just knew he would show up at the greenhouse doors soon, ready to get back to work. By the end of the week, when he didn't show up, her concern grew. She understood she would have to seek him out, and convince him to come back, before he fell too far behind in his studies. She walked down to the college's administration office to get his home address.

"Sure, that's the cutie with the golden, curly hair, isn't it?" the pretty brunette behind the counter said, as she searched the computer records for his name. "He doesn't say much, does he? You know, you're not the first in here trying to get his home phone number... you say you're his mentor?"

"Yes, through the Horticulture program. He hasn't been here all week, and I would like to make sure he is okay," Genevieve said, as she fiddled with the pencil holder on the counter.

The girl ran her finger down the computer screen scanning the names, and smiled just as her finger stopped.

"Daniel Kent, here it is, but I can only give it you, because you are... like... his teacher or something," she said, not hiding her jealousy very well.

Genevieve felt as if she was lying, even though she wasn't. Her ears were getting hot; she just wished the girl would give her the number already.

The girl peered up, scrutinizing Genevieve's face. Then she shrugged, and handed her the print-out of Danny's personal information. Genevieve folded it and stuffed it in her back-pack. The girl raised her eyebrows, like she was about to ask a question, but Genevieve rushed out before the girl could speak again. Why did she feel like a silly school girl, trying to get the number of the most popular boy in school? She knew Danny was attractive, but she hadn't appreciated how many girls pined after him. She wondered if *he* even knew.

She sat in the car staring at the paper, for the better part of ten minutes, vacillating back and forth between driving to his apartment, or letting him work it out in his own time. Her heart told her she needed to go to him, but her head mulled over a million questions. Would it be wrong to go over to his apartment? What would she say to him, when she saw him? Would he push her away again? She started up the car, and gripped the steering wheel with both hands.

He was a friend in need, and she was going to help him.

Help him what? That would be the real challenge.

She pulled up in front of his apartment, but nerves got the better of her. She sat there with her car idling, wondering if she could face him again. She had made things so much worse, by being nosy. If she hadn't started asking questions about his parents, if she hadn't asked what happened to his sister, none of this would have happened. He would be coming to the greenhouse, cracking up over her stupid jokes, and keeping her company in the afternoons. Instead he had disappeared, with apparently no intention of coming back. He probably hated her now.

She turned off the car, and took a deep breath. It was no use sitting outside his apartment, convincing herself of the worst. Whatever he had to say to her could not be any worse than what she was making up in her mind. She opened the door up, sticking one leg out, then two, and next thing she knew she was knocking at his door. No one answered, and she turned around to leave, slightly relieved, but even more worried. Where could he be? Then she heard the deadbolt slide, and the door opened. Out ran an orange and cream cat, who wound around her legs. An arm shot out, scooping up the cat in one fell swoop.

"Gotta watch this one, too many birds to kill, too little time," Danny said, and winked at her.

Genevieve reached out and rubbed the cat under the chin. It instantly started purring, struggling to get out of Danny's hands.

"Sousa, right? Aw, he looks harmless enough."

"The greatest beasts have the ability to appear harmless, so they can charm and bite you, all at the same time," Danny said, not meeting her gaze.

They stood awkwardly for a minute, both of them diverting their nervous attention to Sousa, who was more interested in the birds in the trees than in either of them.

Danny moved aside, and motioned her into the open door. She stepped by him to walk in, brushing past him lightly. The apartment was just like she had imagined. Sure enough, a clean apartment with modern art on the walls. She secretly smiled to herself.

Danny set Sousa down, and looked at Genevieve. She felt almost entranced by his gaze. She glanced down to break the trance, noticing he was barefoot. She had never seen him without shoes on, and it struck her as odd. He had nice feet.

"So, can I get you something to drink?" Danny asked, making her look up sharply.

"Uh, no. Danny, I just wanted to make sure you're okay. I was worried," Genevieve muttered quickly. She glanced at his face, to see if she could read it. "Did I make you mad?"

He turned his head slightly, and crinkled his brow.

"Mad? Wow, that never even occurred to me. I'm okay I guess, after making a fool of myself in front of you. I was too embarrassed to face you this week."

"You didn't make a fool of yourself in front of me! What are you talking about?"

"Geez, Gen, I stood there and cried in front of you! I told you something and broke down," he shouted, an expression of pain lining his face.

She moved closer and took his hand.

"That's making a fool of yourself? Being human? Damn it, Danny, you're human! You have the right to feel things. We all cry, we all hurt. I would be more confused, if you told me about Emily and didn't cry. What happened to you both as children would break most adults, and yet here you stand in front of me, a compassionate, strong man. Who the hell taught you that you didn't have that right to cry?" Genevieve pleaded.

He stared at her with the hurt look of a child on his face, and it dawned on her. His father...

"Your father was an ass. Don't let anything he ever taught, or showed you, be the judge of what kind of man you are. I like who you are. You are real." She gripped his hand tighter. She saw that his inner turmoil was caused by years of being beaten down.

His face eased as the reality dawned on him, what he had been told all his childhood was nothing more than another form of abuse. Tenderness replaced the stress in his face.

"Gen, what did I do to deserve a friend like you in my life?" he asked, hugging her firmly.

She stood back and laughed. "You mowed my lawn."

"That I did, but you already paid me. Too much, I might add."

The tension between them melted away, as they laughed. Danny walked over to the couch to sit down. He patted the seat beside him, and Genevieve came to sit down. For the first time since arriving, she noticed he had classical music playing softly in the background. She leaned back against his shoulder, and sighed.

"You know, Danny, I've really missed you this week. The greenhouse is big and empty, without you messing everything up."

"What do you mean, messing everything up?" he asked, poking her in the ribs.

Genevieve started slightly and sat up.

"I mean, you better get your plants straight soon, or I will have to recommend you repeat the mentor program. I'm tired of re-labeling the plants correctly," she replied, poking him back in the ribs.

He chuckled, nodding his head in agreement. In truth,

they both knew Danny was incredibly bright, and needed very little guidance with anything.

They chatted about school and family, and then Genevieve knew there was a subject she had to broach—no matter how painful it was. She turned to face Danny, looking at him seriously. He looked back at her, knowing what was coming. His eyes met hers, and she could tell he was ready. She cleared her throat, as she thought of the best way to say what needed to be said.

"Danny, I'm begging of you, please don't blame yourself for what happened to Emily. You were just a small child—with no power! Guilt is a self-defeating emotion, and you have come too far in your life, to let it all crash down now," she paused, watching his face to make sure it was okay to continue. "Emily knew her big brother tried to save her. I truly believe that."

"Gen, I have had this week to think over everything, and I know you're right. But there is still a part of me that feels if I had just done something, I could have saved her. Maybe not, maybe it's like some belief that when it's your time, it's your time. When I was a little boy, I would lie in bed and talk to Emily after she died. I would beg her to just come back to me. She never did, and I felt I was being punished for not saving her."

"You thought that?" Genevieve asked incredulously. "Danny, if anything, she didn't come back, because she had had enough of the cruelty of your parents—which you endured for six more years!"

Danny bit his bottom lip, thinking about that possibility. His eyes were distant, going back to the past through an adult's eyes. He got up, and walked over to a stack of books piled up near the stereo. He opened the cover of one, and started flipping through the pages. A tattered picture fluttered out, and Danny caught it before it hit the ground.

He silently handed it to Genevieve. She peered into a faded picture of a newborn baby.

"That's Emily," Danny whispered hoarsely. "That's the only picture of her anywhere. The hospital gave all the parents a picture of their new baby, when they left the hospital the first time. After she died, I snuck in and stole this from the album."

Genevieve peered closely at the picture. The baby in it had delicate rosebud lips, and curly, blond hair like Danny's. Of course, she looked like most newborns, with a puffy face and swollen eyes, but Genevieve could imagine what a gorgeous baby she must have been. She handed the picture back to Danny, then stood up and kissed his cheek.

"Danny, Emily is still with you. Only her body isn't, but her soul lives on."

The phone rang sharply, and they stood there frozen. She motioned to Danny to answer it. He reluctantly picked up the receiver and started talking. Genevieve stood for a moment to see if it would be a short call, but obviously he was going to be stuck on there for awhile. She glanced at her watch and saw it was getting late. Joe would worry if she didn't come soon. She waved to Danny that she was leaving. He put his hand over the receiver, turning his attention to her.

"Gen, thank you...for everything. I'll see you Monday?" he asked hopefully.

"I'll be there. I have been waiting on you to show those baby blues all week. Please come back, Danny, I miss you."

"I will, baby. With bells on," he said, and touched two of his fingers to his brow with a little wave, like he always did.

She grinned back at him and left, shutting the door quietly behind her. Once back in her car, she thought about everything which had transpired within the last week. It never ceased to amaze her how everyone had a story to tell, but most were just never given the chance. Her life was pretty rosy in comparison. Every time she was about to complain about the price of milk, or a run in her stocking, she would try and remind herself she was one of the lucky ones in life.

The lights were on at home, and Joe was in the kitchen whistling, when Genevieve walked in. He turned and smiled at her. Becca was upstairs playing her music way too loud, and they both looked up as they heard the floor boards creaking under her dancing feet.

Joe came over and wrapped his arms around Genevieve. He smelled nice, of pipe smoke. She leaned against him, yawning. Sometimes it was just so nice to have someone you could come home to. At times, Joe was like the father she never had. He was calm and understanding... and trusting.

Why then, did that make her feel so bad?

Chapter Ten

It had come to an end.

Genevieve ran her finger through the spilled potting soil on the counter, and glimpsed around the greenhouse. In more ways than one, this had been her sanctuary over the last four years. After that first indecisive year at college, she had come here and never looked back. Now with graduation looming over her, it was not only time to say good-bye to college, but also to the greenhouse... and in too many ways, to Danny.

He would always be her friend, but she feared they would never have the connection of being away from the rest of the world together, like they had in the greenhouse.

As if conjured up solely by her thoughts, Danny strode

in, and set his bag down by the door. Without saying a
word, he strolled over to the other counter and sat down,
never even looking in her direction. With his back to her,
he opened his notebook and started to write.

Genevieve was shocked by his distance, and wondered
if she had done something to offend him. Her mind raced
through what they had talked about in the previous days.
Nothing stood out which would cause hurt feelings, that she
could think of.

"Danny, is everything okay?"

"Just banner, Genevieve," he replied coldly, not looking
up.

What had she done? Why was he so mad at her? She
walked over to where he was sitting, and put her hand on
his shoulder. He tightened up and pulled away, focusing on
the notebook in front of him. He was mad at her! Her
heart jumped in her chest, as she let her hands drop.

She stepped away from him, her feelings hurt, and her
head befuddled. She picked up a pack of labels on the
counter, and started to fill them out. She had to label and
pack the seeds away for next year, so the incoming students
would be able to find their way around her... er... *the*
greenhouse. She just couldn't get focused, and knew she
needed to do something about Danny.

"Danny, please come over here and help me label these
packages, so we can pack them away today," she tried to
say in her best mentor voice.

At first, it seemed that he hadn't heard her because he
kept writing with his head down. She was about to repeat
herself, when he stood up slowly, and closed his book with
a bang. She jumped at the sound, and tried to regain her
composure.

Danny came and stood beside her, but would not look
over at her. She handed him a list and a pack of labels,

which he started to fill out at a furious pace. It was like he was a totally different person, and it frightened Genevieve more than a little.

They worked for the better part of an hour like this; all the while Genevieve was trying to figure out why Danny wouldn't speak to her. She remembered back again, and although he had been quieter and joking less over the last few weeks, she had assumed it was due to their finals.

Absentmindedly, she reached out blindly with her hand for another page of labels, accidentally brushing his hand with hers. He jerked his hand away, as if she was on fire. Genevieve could not believe it had come to this.

"Danny! What is it? What have I done?" she cried out.

He slammed his fist down on the counter, making pens and seeds jump everywhere.

"Damn it, Gen, as if you really don't know?" he yelled back, throwing his hands out in disgust.

Then staring at his hands like he didn't know what to do with them, he ran them through his hair making it stick up wildly.

She stared at him with round eyes, confused. She noticed it didn't look like he had slept in weeks. His eyes were red rimmed and puffy, his face obviously filled with tension. She took a step towards him, and he took a step back.

"Please, Danny, I don't know what's going on," she whispered desperately.

She took another step towards him, but he put his hand up to keep her back. She took another step towards him, and he backed up into the counter.

"Genevieve, don't... " he pleaded, his eyes filled with pain.

She took another step towards him and now stood only inches away. His whole body was rigid; every muscle in him seemed to be tensed.

"Please, tell me what's going on. We are such good friends! Why don't you want to be near me?" Genevieve asked, grabbing his hand.

"Gen, don't you know… " his voice trailed off.

She stared up into his eyes, and then she knew. She knew what her heart had been telling her all along. The attraction between them, although temporarily put away over the last year, was as strong as ever and tore at each of them trying to be free.

As if gravity had taken hold, they came together in an instant, their bodies melding into one form. He pressed his large mouth against hers. Genevieve could feel the gentleness of his lips on hers, and the hardness of his hands on her back, as she clutched his arms. His tongue tickled her lips, and a soft moan escaped her. He tasted salty, from the heat of the greenhouse, and smelled of the earth.

In that moment, Genevieve felt like all her years of longing and searching had found their resting place. Their lips broke apart and he hid his face in her hair, his breath coming in short rasps. She laid her forehead on his neck, and caught her breath. She felt them sink together, until their knees hit the floor. Their bodies were pressed against each other, their arms intertwined, holding on for dear life.

"Danny, I …I mean we can't. I can't…" she half-heartedly protested.

She wanted to just forget all the reasons why not, but she knew she couldn't.

He sighed and loosened his grip on her waist.

"I know, Gen. I know. It's wrong."

He sat back and pulled her onto his lap, her back against him. They huddled together on the floor, just listening to each other's breathing. She so badly wanted to turn around and tell Danny they should just run away together, but her mind kept going back to Joe and Becca. She loved Joe and Becca; they were her family, her world. She couldn't betray them, or the life they shared. Danny picked up a strand of Genevieve's hair, and twirled it around his finger.

"Do you still love Joe?" he asked, as if he had been reading her mind.

"I do...yes. He is my husband, my friend, and the father of my child."

"Do you love me, then?" he asked quietly, his body tensed, waiting for her response.

Genevieve mulled this over in her mind, but the answer had been there all along.

"Yes, Danny I do. I guess, I have for quite sometime," she said, leaning her head back against him.

He brushed her hair off of her neck, and kissed her shoulder. A faint sigh escaped her lips.

"Do you want me, like I want you?" he asked.

"Oh, honey, you have no idea how badly I want you! I have been with you so many times in my dreams," she answered, with conviction.

"Where does that leave us then?" he said, more as a statement than a question.

Where did that leave them?

Genevieve knew where, and she knew Danny did, too. No matter how they felt, their roads were already laid out. At least hers was. Life had already taken her someplace, and she couldn't go back.

She turned to face him, and took both his hands in hers. Her heart started pounding rapidly, as she took a deep breath. She looked down at their clasped hands, his strong long ones and her thin delicate ones.

Give me the strength to do this.

"Danny, I made a commitment to another person many years ago, and in that commitment we created a child. I'm indebted to the choice I made. I love my husband and my daughter. I love you too, but they came first. So, them I have to stay faithful," she whispered.

"I understand," Danny said sadly. "But, Gen, I will always love you, which will never change."

"Oh Danny, even if I wasn't married, I'm thirteen years older than you..."

He tried to cut her off, but she pressed her fingers to his lips.

"I know you think it doesn't matter, but you have your whole life ahead of you. You will meet someone your age, who will steal your heart. You will get married and have a family... things I can't offer you."

"Gen, those things don't matter, and no matter how much older you are than me, our souls are the same. I have been drawn to you since I was a kid, and yet I have to walk away over and over again?"

"I'm sorry... I guess our timing is bad, Danny. There's nothing we can do about that. We can still be friends... I know, I know... the old 'we can still be friends' speech, but it's not like that. I need you in my life. Over the last year, I have made the best friend I have ever had. I just can't have you in everyway that you... that we both want."

She sat back away from him, and they regarded each other for a long time. All too quickly, the sadness in his face was replaced by his smooth happy-go-lucky look. It was like watching the theatre faces change from one to another. Genevieve realized he was putting walls up, to avoid being hurt.

Out of desperation to prevent his hurting, she leaned forward and kissed him. He pulled back in surprise, and then let the emotion take him. They kissed each other fiercely, not wanting to let up and let reality in. Danny pushed her away slightly and looked into her eyes pleading.

"Gen, please don't go!"

His words snapped her back to common sense. She stood up so fast she knocked some pots off the counter. He grabbed them before they hit the floor, and stood up to put them on the counter. He stared at the pots, not wanting to meet her eyes and see the end coming. Genevieve reached out and touched the scar on his arm, wishing she didn't have to be the one to say good-bye. She stepped forward and embraced him closely, knowing it was time.

"I'm sorry, I have to go," she murmured.

He sighed, but she could feel him nod slightly.

"I know, baby, but what am I going to do here without you next year?"

"Well don't kill everything, that's the first thing," she chuckled.

She could feel his body relax and then start shaking with laughter. That broke the tension and they let go of each other.

"And the other thing, Danny, please don't close yourself off from the world, because you don't want to be hurt."

He flinched when she said this.

She paused and went on, "Please meet some people; the right person is probably out there looking for you right now. You deserve a girl who is just yours, one that can give you a family and a life."

He shook his head when she said this.

Genevieve knew he would close himself off, if she didn't make him see that good things can happen too. Even though she was attracted to Danny, she would never have traded her family, or the experiences she had with Joe over the years. She wanted Danny to have those same things in his future.

"Danny, please just promise me you will try, life has so much to offer!"

"I will promise you that, if you can promise me one thing," he said huskily.

"Anything."

"Just come back to me. Some how, some way."

Chapter Eleven

It was amazing how a year changed things. Genevieve glanced around at her ever-growing nursery, and smiled. After graduation, she worked in a nursery department of a local discount store, but she didn't like the lack of care of the plants. More often than not, they were throwing away dead plants, or marking down flowers that shouldn't have even been sold. She watched people buying the cheap plants she knew would die, probably before they would even get them into the ground. She quit one day, when her manager refused to let her tell a customer that fact.

She saved every penny of what she made, and by the following spring she purchased enough startup supplies to start her own nursery. Earthy Hands Nursery, she called it.

Joe gave her the land, which was adjacent to his construction equipment yard. She mostly dealt in business landscaping, although a fair share of the nursery's income came from homeowners.

The construction company had already put in an order, for when they were ready to landscape the new agriculture building they were completing. Business was starting to pour in, and she hardly had time to breathe, much less think about anything else.

Tonight was different though. Maureen had called and invited her to the graduation at the college. Maureen remembered Genevieve had mentored Danny, and he was graduating that evening. Genevieve at first thought it wasn't wise to go, but also knew she couldn't stay away. She was so proud of him, and wanted to see him accept his diploma. Well… she really just wanted to see *him*.

In the past year, he had crossed her mind often. She wondered if he ever thought of her. Sometimes she would be working, hands in the dirt, and it was as if she could feel him thinking of her. She'd look up, and see he wasn't actually standing there. It made her question if he was picturing her in his mind, at that exact moment. Secretly she hoped he did, because he crossed her mind so often. Maybe, in another lifetime…

She wanted to bring him something special as a graduation gift, and hoped he wouldn't be to upset she showed up. They hadn't spoken since that emotional day in the greenhouse, although she had seen him in the back of the auditorium at her graduation. He had watched her then, but was gone by the time the ceremony let out.

She was still pondering what to get Danny later that day, when Joe came into the nursery.

"Hi, darling," he said, as he leaned down to smell a rosebush. "Almost ready to head home?"

"Oh, Joe, I forgot to tell you! Maureen called, and wants me to come to the college graduation tonight. Some of our mentor students from last year are graduating. I figured I'd better finish up here first, and then get over there."

"No problem. Well, I'm going to swing by the school to pick Becca up. Maybe I'll take her out shopping, or something, tonight."

Joe and Becca had been trying to keep ties, throughout her tumultuous preteen years. Now that she was thirteen, it was getting tougher. Genevieve saw how badly Becca just wanted to be close to her dad, but her hormones and emotions pushed him away. Joe tried, but he couldn't truly understand the turmoil Becca's body was going through. More often than not, he said the wrong thing, at the wrong time, to her.

"That's a great idea! Hey, while you are out, she needs some new bras," Genevieve said, and chuckled as she saw Joe wince.

"Uh... I-I don't... "

"Just kidding, Joe! Dinner and some shoes would be just fine."

"Oh, good, I can do that," Joe sighed, relieved. He came over, and kissed Genevieve on the top of the head

"I probably stink," Genevieve said, laughing.

"No more than I do. Are you planning to go to graduation like that?" he asked, pointing at her dirty shirt and knees.

She peered down and grimaced. She hadn't thought of that.

"No, I suppose not. I guess I will swing home, and grab a shower first... otherwise Maureen will make me sit outside!"

"Well, babe, I'd better go get our girl, before she throws

a fit outside the school. See you tonight," he said, giving her a quick peck on the lips.

Then he was gone, and she was alone. This was her favorite time of the day. Everyone else headed home, and she could sit with her plants and think. She swept up the floor of the shop, and watered the outside plants. As she locked up the gates, she realized she was running short on time if she wanted to make the graduation. She hurried out to her car, and drove a bit too fast home.

The house was quiet and dark. If Joe and Becca had been home, they had already left to go shopping. She went up to the bathroom, and slipped her clothes off. She caught a glimpse of herself in the mirror, and smiled. Not too bad for thirty-five. All the work at the nursery had tightened her muscles, and slimmed her down quite a bit. Sure, she had a few smile lines, and a few unnoticeable grays, but all in all she looked pretty good.

She climbed in the shower, sighing as the hot water relaxed her muscles. She could feel her hair tickling the small of her back, and hadn't known it had grown so long. She hadn't paid attention to much in the last year. She affectionately referred to herself as pigpen most days, and rarely put on as much as a dab of makeup.

After the shower, she rooted around in her closet, searching for something to wear which wasn't stained from the nursery. She finally chose a shimmering, silver, silk top, and black slacks. With her golden red hair, she had to admit she looked gorgeous. She applied some light makeup, and let her hair fall into its natural waves. She peered back and grinned.

A quick glance at the clock revealed she was dangerously close to being locked out of the graduation, and she grabbed her purse. She was going to be late, but she had one more stop to make before she got to the graduation. Maureen was going to kill her!

When she at last arrived at the graduation, they were already up to the letter "F" in the names. She slipped in beside Maureen, who rolled her eyes back at her. Genevieve elbowed her, and grinned. Maureen just shook her head.

Genevieve scanned the graduates until she saw Danny. Seeing him caught her breath. He didn't appear to notice her, so she just spent her time staring at him. He didn't seem to be looking at anyone in the audience, she grasped he probably had no one there to see him graduate. Her heart ached at the thought of it. At least she was here.

When they finally got to the "K"s, Genevieve found she was holding her breath. She heard the speaker call his name monotonously. Danny rose and sauntered across the stage, shaking the hands of the staff. As he turned to go back to his seat, Genevieve swore he looked right at her. A tingle ran up her neck, and she dropped her eyes down quickly. She fidgeted with her fingers, hoping no one had noticed her reaction.

The rest of the ceremony, Danny didn't look at her once; he just kept his eyes glazed forward. Genevieve thought seriously about just leaving quietly when it was over, but she had the present she bought him. Patting her purse to make sure the present was still safe and sound, she breathed in deeply and relaxed back in her seat.

"Well, that's it," Maureen said, when the final speeches were made. She pinched Genevieve on the arm. "Come with me, I have some Horticulture students who just graduated... maybe you could give jobs to?"

"Ha! That's the real reason you invited me huh, Mo? Lining up jobs for your students, are you?"

"But of course, so shut up, and come on!" Maureen said, dragging Genevieve by the arm.

They mingled with the graduated Horticulture students, at the reception. Genevieve handed out quite a few business cards among them. The nursery was starting to pick up enough, where she would need to hire some people as managers, so she wouldn't have to do everything. She was pleased with the potential employees she met.

One boy in particular, named Rogan Kelley, seemed to know his stuff, and had a clear head on his shoulders. He seemed to be followed by a herd of pretty young girls, though, which made Genevieve question his dedication. Even so, he left an impression on her, so she thought she'd be calling him in a few weeks for an interview.

Maureen wandered off, and was no where to be seen. Exasperated by her flighty friend, Genevieve decided to take the time to wander through the gardens at the college. She had planted so much in them; she wanted to see if they were getting as much care and attention, as they had while she was there.

She peered around one more time for Maureen, and then slipped out into the night. She hadn't seen Danny, and wondered if he had left directly after the ceremony. Maybe he had seen her, and didn't want another awkward meeting. Shrugging, she headed out, and enjoyed the stroll to the gardens as the fragrances led her way. Someone had definitely been keeping the gardens going.

Genevieve walked silently down the paths, stopping and sniffing the flowers on her way. Surprisingly, she found she was alone on such a beautiful night in the garden. Then again, unless some young couple had come to find a quiet make-out spot, the gardens were often empty in the evenings. She liked the feeling of being solitary in such a magical place, and hoped no one would disturb her visit.

In the center of the gardens, was a fountain surrounded by benches. When Genevieve was a student, she would sit there and study. She decided that a visit there tonight would calm her nerves from being near Danny again. She made her way through the paths, which were built in the shape of a round maze, to the center. In the evening light, the water flowing out of the fountain sparkled like tiny diamonds. She walked around the fountain, tracing her finger along the cool wet marble.

Suddenly, she sensed she wasn't alone. A figure shifted on one of the benches, on the far side of the fountain. She peeked around, and saw someone sitting on the bench, leaning forward with his head in his hands. As she focused in, she recognized those blond curls.

"Danny?" she asked, as she sat down beside him.

He looked up, and smiled at her wearily.

"I knew you would come."

Chapter Twelve

"**Oh**, you know me, just can't stay away," Genevieve said sarcastically, nudging Danny with her elbow.

He gazed up at her and chuckled softly. He leaned back, and regarded her for a second. The moonlight cast a delicate glow on her.

"Wow, you look stunning!"

"Gee, thanks. I clean up nice. You should have seen me a couple of hours ago—head to toe dirt and grime."

"You would have looked stunning then, too," he replied honestly. "So, how's the nursery going?"

"Oh, you heard about that? It's great! My dream come true."

"Gen, I still know what's going on in your life. I didn't

fall off the face of the Earth, when I walked out of the greenhouse that day, you know," Danny muttered bitterly.

Genevieve flushed with embarrassment; she should have kept in touch.

"Danny, I know you didn't. I wanted to stop by and visit, but it just seemed so..."

"Awkward," he finished for her.

She nodded, and half-smiled at him. He looked at her, unblinking. This was going to be harder than she thought. Danny sometimes was like a ship out in the middle of the ocean, unreachable.

"I'm sorry," she whispered, and took his hand. It was warm, and she was relieved when he curled his fingers around hers.

"I know... me too."

The water from the fountain gurgled soothingly. They sat there in silence, enjoying the quiet of the night and the serenity of the gardens. If only life could be just like this very moment. Unfettered from life's stresses and demands. It was always like that for Genevieve when she was with Danny.

"The gardens look beautiful. I wonder who has been working in them this year," Genevieve wondered aloud.

"I have."

"You? But you are a Naturalist, not a Horticulturist. How'd that come about?"

"I asked Maureen if I could. She thought it would be alright."

"Oh," Genevieve mumbled. She thought of her and Danny, working side-by-side last year in the gardens, and wondered if that's why he had kept the gardens up this year.

"Yeah, it was because of you," he whispered, reading her mind. "You know, Gen, you're the best friend I ever had, and everyday I hoped you would come by and see what was going on, down at the greenhouse. You never did. I figured I blew it last year. But no matter what, I don't want to lose you as a friend."

"You won't, we'll figure out a way. Oh I have something for you!" Genevieve pulled the box out of her purse.

She handed it clumsily to Danny, who stared at it in surprise.

"Open it now. I want to explain it to you."

He gently unpeeled the tape, and slid the wrapping off a blue box. He gently opened the box and pulled out a silver watch. His eyebrows rose as he looked at Genevieve.

"Gen, this is too nice."

"No, it's not, it's just right. I wanted to get you something special for your graduation, and this seemed perfect. Turn it over."

He flipped the watch over, and peered at the back. As he read what Genevieve had engraved, his eyes glistened with tears he held back.

> *Dearest Danny,*
> *Love crosses all*
> *time and bounds…*
> *Forever with you,*
> *Genevieve and Emily*

"I hope it wasn't too presumptuous—you know to include Emily… it just felt right."

"No, not at all," he whispered huskily. "It's incredibly perfect. No one has ever… "

"Shhh, I'm just someone who does."

Danny leaned in, and drew her in close to him. He smelled like spicy aftershave, and felt even better. She pulled away to take the watch from his hand. She unclasped it, and put it around his wrist. He turned his wrist from side to side, once it was on. The watch face caught the moonlight.

Standing up, he took her hand. She rose, and they started walking slowly down the paths. She wanted to ask him about his life, and tell him about hers. Was he seeing someone? Was he going to stay around, or apply for a job elsewhere? Did he ever think of her, like she thought of him?

"So, how is life treating you?" she finally asked.

He shrugged and looked away uncomfortably.

"Alright, I guess. Got a job offer from the Nebraska State Game and Parks."

"That's great! Will you take it?"

"If I can work at Chadron State Park, I will," he replied, smiling down at her.

"That's good. And anything else going on in your life?" she asked tentatively.

He let go of her hand and sighed. He turned to face her. She could tell he was going to say something she didn't want to hear.

"Gen, I have something to tell you, but first I need to ask you a question."

"Sure, what is it?"

"Other than being friends, is there any other future for us?" He watched her seriously.

Genevieve blushed, and looked away.

"Danny, I wish I could say something different, because my heart wants me to. But no. I'm married, and have a family. I love you... and would do almost anything for you. In another lifetime and another place, I believe we would be meant to be. However, we are here and now, and I made my choices. Besides, I am now thirty-five years old, and you are only twenty-two. You have a life waiting for you. A wife, children, experiences. I have done all those things, and really just want to get up in the morning, and stick my hands in dirt, then go home at night and kiss my husband and daughter good-night. Anything else my desires lead me to, I just can't have."

Danny shook his head slightly.

"As far as the age thing, stop bringing it up. It doesn't matter to me. The other things I can understand, and respect, but age is just a number."

"Oh, only when you are twenty-two! Then wrinkles and grays come, and stretch marks after babies, and... oh, Danny, there is just so much for you out in this world. Some old woman is *not* what you need."

"Gen, you're no old woman, never be mistaken on that. There isn't a girl out there who can hold a candle to you. Besides, in the end we all get old anyway. And by the way, I'll be twenty-three next month."

"True, but the experiences in getting there need to happen. You need to find someone your age to be with, to marry, and to have babies with."

"So you say. I would rather find someone to travel with, drink coffee with…and play in the dirt with," he replied, and winked at her.

"Pipe dreams, baby, all pipe dreams," Genevieve said, laughing.

"I do have something to tell you, though…" Danny started to say, when Genevieve heard a female voice calling his name.

Danny's eyes got wide, and he grimaced, as he turned towards the approaching voice.

Out of the shadows, a beautiful brunette stepped. She looked at Danny and Genevieve's clasped hands, and fire shot through her eyes. As she approached and saw who Genevieve was, her faced relaxed and she smiled.

"Oh, you must be just Genevieve," she said over-sweetly, sizing Genevieve up.

Genevieve nodded quickly, feeling her ears getting hot.

"Danny says you are like the sister he never had. I'm Stacey, Danny's girlfriend," the brunette announced.

Genevieve stared over at Danny, confused. She let her hand drop to her side. A girlfriend? The sister he *never had*? What was going on? Danny's face was red, and he didn't make eye contact with Genevieve.

Just Genevieve?

"Um, yes I am Genevieve. I was Danny's mentor last year, we ran into each other in the gardens. Uh... it's nice to meet you."

Stacey leaned in and kissed Danny on the lips, eyeing Genevieve as she did so. She grabbed his hand tight in hers, and then noticed the watch he was wearing. She lifted up his wrist, to take a closer look at it.

"Wow, that's gorgeous. Must have cost a fortune! Is it from you?" she asked Genevieve, almost accusingly.

Genevieve stood there, feeling so stupid and out of place. Her head moved up in down stiffly. If she could just get out of there! Her mind was racing about as fast as her heart.

"Fancy gift for someone who is just a *friend*," Stacey said, with the emphasis on the word friend.

Genevieve felt anger rising up in her.

"Oh, but don't forget," she seethed. "I'm more like the sister he never had."

Genevieve turned on her heel, and stormed off. In her indignation, she took a wrong turn, and got lost in the maze of the garden. She turned around, trying to figure her way out, but managed to get even more lost. She stomped her foot, and kicked a statue along the path.

"Ow, damn it!" she cursed, grabbing her throbbing foot.

She hopped around for a minute, when she started to lose her balance. She flailed out searching for something to grab onto, her hand landing on something warm. She glared up to see Danny's apologetic face. She snatched her hand away from his arm, and started to walk off.

"Wait, Gen! Let me explain," he called after her.

She spun around to confront him.

"You know, I don't know if I should be more upset for me, or for Emily. The sister you never had? You have a sister! And it's not me!"

"Gen, she doesn't know about Emily, because it's not something I share with just anybody. I only told you! Geez, Gen, make up your mind! You pushed me away, and told me to find someone, and then you get mad when I did. You broke my heart, told me to fix it, and then you keep breaking it!"

They faced each other, breathing heavy and glaring. Calmness began to replace Genevieve's rage, and she pondered over what he had said. She realized she *was* playing him like a yo-yo. She had to cut the strings, to let him live his own life. She wasn't thinking clearly, or being fair.

"You're right, Danny. I can't give you what you want. The only way to give you your freedom is to walk out of your life… in every way, for good. But please, don't push Emily out. She's your sister, and you need to honor her, by telling people you love about her life. I will always care about you. To do that, though, I need to take myself out of the equation. Good-bye."

She turned and ran, before he could say anything back to her. Tears streamed down her face, as she made it out of the garden. She ran all the way to her car. It was over. Danny had moved on, and now she needed to plant her feet back where they belonged. She wasn't a silly school girl anymore.

Before her whole world came crashing down, because of her stupidity, she knew she had to go back to the family she had chosen.

Joe.

Joe.

His name guided her home, to the safety of his faithful arms.

Chapter Thirteen

There was definitely a second line appearing. Genevieve picked up the pregnancy test off the bathroom counter. She shook it like a thermometer, hoping to make the, very definitely appearing, second line disappear. It didn't. Well, that was that then. She'd have to tell Joe, who would be pretty thrilled—he always wanted more children. Maybe not when he was in his fifties, but better late than never, Genevieve supposed.

Genevieve leaned against the counter, and took a deep breath. True to her word, in the garden a few weeks ago, she had not spoken to, or seen, Danny again. That night she had rushed home, distraught and confused. Remarkably, Joe had been up and in a good mood, instead of crashed out in his easy-chair by nine, like he usually was. Genevieve had collapsed next to him on the couch, and laid her head on his shoulder.

Joe had told her of the evening he and Becca had shared. It had sounded like they had made some headway in their father-daughter relationship. Then they had started talking about when Becca was a baby, and laughed how much life had changed since then. One thing had led to another, and they found themselves holding hands, as they ascended the stairs to their bedroom. For the first time in years, Joe and Genevieve had shared real passion. It was like their first year together.

"And look where it got me," Genevieve muttered, and rubbed her still flat stomach. "Thirty-five and pregnant."

Genevieve puttered around the house, waiting for Joe to arrive home with Becca. When she heard the car doors slam, she broke out in a cold sweat. This was it. Their life was about to be turned on its head. She wiped her sweaty palms on her jeans, and met them at the door.

"Hiya, babe. Home early from the nursery today?" Joe asked, and kissed her on the lips. He pulled his head back, and looked hard at her. "What is it? What's wrong?"

"Um, Joe. I have something to share. But, maybe you'd better sit down for this one. Becca you can stay too, since this involves you."

Joe and Becca looked at each other, with matching confusion. They slowly moved over to the couch, and sat down. Genevieve sat in a chair across from them, and took a ragged breath.

"This is totally unexpected, and I know it will come as a shock, but it can be a good thing... I guess. You know I haven't been feeling good lately," Genevieve stammered.

Joe got an expression of distress on his face; he was thinking it was something really bad.

"Oh, no! Joe, it's nothing like cancer, or anything like that. I'm pregnant!"

The range of emotions that shot over Joe's face in a split second, almost made Genevieve laugh. Shock, confusion, disbelief, more confusion, and then a smile. He got up, and grabbed her up out of the chair. He kissed her hard on the mouth, his whisker rubbing her chin.

"Oh my, honey! I can't believe it! This is something…" he said, shaking his head in amazement.

"Gee, Mom, Dad, I didn't know you had it in you still," Becca said quietly, from the couch.

Genevieve looked over at Becca, who didn't seem necessarily happy. After all, Becca had been an only child for thirteen years. Genevieve walked over, and sat down beside Becca on the couch. She put an arm around Becca's shoulders.

"It'll be alright sweetie. You'll see," Genevieve consoled.

Becca nodded, but kept her head down. Thirteen was a tough year in normal circumstances, and adding a new baby sibling was probably not top on Becca's list.

"I know, Mom. I'll adjust. Can I go to my room?"

"Sure, baby. If you need me, just holler, okay?"

Becca silently rose and headed upstairs. Genevieve knew Becca would come around, but fourteen years age difference would probably always leave an emotional gap between her and the baby. At least as adults, when Genevieve and Joe had since passed away, they would have each other.

Joe came over from behind, and placed his hands on her belly. She laid her hands over his, and smiled. Maybe, just maybe, they could regain the spark they once had. They certainly had a few weeks ago, and Genevieve hadn't seen Joe this happy in years. He and Becca were finally getting along; financially they were more than set, and now a new baby.

"Thank you, babe, for this," Joe whispered in her ear.

"Well, it takes two, but you're welcome. Just remember to be this gracious, when I'm puking and demanding weird food in the middle of the night!"

"I was last time, wasn't I?"

"Yeah, Joe, you were. You have always been so good to me," Genevieve sighed.

He had always been good to her. They didn't argue much, and he had supported her every time she wanted to pursue a dream. She knew many women didn't have it half that good.

Joe went over and turned on an oldies radio station. He put his hand out to her, and she accepted. He drew her close, as they danced smoothly to a slow song. In that moment, Genevieve knew where she belonged. Right there in Joe's arms. They danced through a few songs. When Joe turned her, she caught a glimpse of Becca sitting on the stairs watching them. She winked at Becca, who smiled back, and then crept back up the stairs to her room.

The next morning as Genevieve leaned over the toilet dry-heaving; she knew it was still worth it. This baby would come into a close-knit loving family, and life would be good. She sat back, pushing her sweaty hair out of her face. Joe came in behind her, and handed her a cool glass of water. She smiled gratefully up at him, and took a few sips. No sooner had they hit her stomach, she was leaning back over the toilet puking it back up.

She waved Joe away, and crawled into the hallway. She sat against the wall, placing her head between her knees. She felt a body sit down next to her, and peered up into Becca's concerned face.

"Welcome to pregnancy," Genevieve said wryly.

"I am *never* having children," Becca exclaimed.

"Oh, and baby, this is the easy part."

Genevieve felt Becca's arm slide around her shoulders. For some reason, this was a great source of comfort. Genevieve kept her head between her knees, which seemed to help. Usually, the nausea passed by mid-morning, and then she could head to the nursery. Becca was out of the school for the summer, keeping busy working at the nursery as well. This would help Genevieve greatly until the morning sickness passed. By the end of the summer she would be in her second trimester, and feeling much better. Hopefully.

Once Genevieve could stand up, without having to run to the bathroom every five minutes, she went downstairs and ate a piece of dry toast. Joe had already left for work, but had left her a love note on the counter. She beamed when she read it, and wrote a quick one back—in case he got home before she did.

Becca came down in her jeans and work t-shirt, with her long straight brown hair tied back with a piece of cord. Genevieve couldn't believe looking at her; there wasn't too much difference anymore between the two of them. Although Genevieve was fairly tall at five-foot-seven, Becca was already her height, and still growing. Joe was six foot tall, so Becca must have taken after him. She was so gorgeous! How she could look so much like Joe, and yet be so feminine and beautiful, Genevieve couldn't figure. Really, Becca didn't look much like Genevieve at all. She even had her dad's beautiful light hazel eyes, with just a hint of green.

Genevieve placed her hand on her belly, wondering if this baby would look like her or Joe. It didn't matter, but she always wondered the *whats* and *ifs* when she was pregnant. She wouldn't mind one of her children at least looking a little bit like her.

"You think it will be a boy or girl?" Becca asked out of the blue, staring at Genevieve's stomach.

"Oh, I don't know. Either will be great. I mean, look at you, I couldn't ask for anything better!"

Becca rolled her eyes, but a small grin peeked at the corners of her mouth.

"Well, I hope it's a boy," she said matter-of-factly.

"Why?"

"I don't know. I guess, because I like the idea of protecting my little brother, and doing stuff with him."

"Would it be so different with a sister? You could do those same things with a girl."

"Yeah, I know, but somehow I just picture my little brother. That's what I want."

Genevieve didn't reply, but thought about that. She, too, could see Becca holding the hand of a little brother. In her mind, she could see an older Becca walking up the street towards school, holding the hand of a red-headed little boy. She shook her head and laughed. Already she was creating not only a gender, but a whole look.

"Can I name my little brother?" Becca asked forcefully.

Genevieve's eyebrows went up.

"Well, if it's a boy, and your Dad is okay with it, *and* you don't want to name it something like Dustbunny or Moonstar, I don't have a problem with it," Genevieve replied.

Becca walked over to Genevieve, and bent down to her stomach.

"Hello, Ben," she whispered.

Ben. Genevieve liked the sound of that. And somehow she knew that's who would arrive when the time came.

Chapter Fourteen

Genevieve grunted as she pushed herself up from squatting to check the leaves on a Dwarf Burning Bush at the nursery. The leaves were starting to turn red, which meant summer was definitely over, and fall was well under way. Of course, her ever growing stomach could tell her as much.

Five months pregnant, and way huger than she had been with Becca. Although, back then she was only twenty-three and now she was... well, quite a bit older. This pregnancy had brought its new forms of concerns, too. More tests, because she was over thirty-five, and Joe was over fifty. The ultrasounds had come back good, and the amniocentesis had been clear. It had also confirmed what

Becca and Genevieve had known along. This baby was a boy!

Joe had loved the name Benjamin, and was even more tickled Becca had chosen it. They agreed on Joseph as a middle name, after Joe. Benjamin Joseph Howard. It had a nice ring to it. Genevieve rubbed her belly, and felt a kick in return. The morning sickness had passed quickly after she started her second trimester. Now, it was just her ever growing body she had to deal with.

She gazed around the nursery. Soon, they would only have living Christmas trees and decorations for sale. Benjamin would be born during Genevieve's down time. She looked forward to her time getting to know him, during those quiet months.

She silently thanked Maureen, for introducing her to some of the graduating Horticulture students in the spring. She had hired three of them, and they were doing a phenomenal job keeping the place running. Becca had done more than her fair share in the summer, but she was back in school now, and had started eighth grade. Becca would turn fourteen right after Christmas. It was such a crazy time of year.

Rogan, one of the graduates she had hired, was making his way through the shrubs towards her. He was grinning ear to ear.

Becca had been starry-eyed all summer, working with Rogan. Genevieve had to work to keep her busy and away from him. He was a dashing young man, with dark hair and blackish-brown eyes to match. Genevieve felt for Becca, being seven and half years younger than Rogan, and no more than a child in his eyes. Rogan always treated her like a kid. More than once, Genevieve had seen the hurt in her eyes.

"Mrs. Howard, the new hotel on the highway would like

to buy most of our remaining shrubs, but they wanted to know if planting them in October was a good idea?"

"Absolutely. It's easier on them to be planted when they have gone dormant. They won't grow, of course, over the winter, but they will really do well in the spring. Hold on, let me talk to them."

"The owner is out front, maybe you can help him with landscaping as well," Rogan said, and pointed over to a rather rotund man who was standing near the gates.

Genevieve approached the man, and he stared uncomfortably at her pregnant belly. Even in this day and age, some people thought a pregnant woman should be home knitting booties.

"Good afternoon. I'm Genevieve, the owner of the nursery. I understand you would like some assistance, in purchasing and landscaping shrubs?"

"Uh, well, yeah. I just opened the Stop Inn Motel, up on the highway. I'd like some bushes to block off the highway, also for around the motel itself. I need a lot, and nobody has any left around here. So, I guess you are it," he said, unconvinced.

"Pretty much, sir. I can more than suit your needs. Planting soon would be a good idea, and I can give you, say, fifteen percent off on my remaining shrubs. One of our team can also help you in your landscaping design...free of charge," Genevieve said with authority.

The man raised his eyebrows, impressed. "You've got a deal!" he said, shaking her hand a little too hard.

Genevieve was pleased. With selling the shrubs, and not getting the Christmas items in until the first of November, she would have a couple of weeks off her feet.

"Well, then let's go inside my office, and write up the paperwork."

After Mr. Stubbs, as she learned his name was, had left,

she leaned back in her chair and smiled. She always liked setting people like that on their ear. A little lesson in open-mindedness never hurt anyone. She would have Rogan go out to set the bushes over the weekend. Then she could hang her "back November 15" sign in the window.

Genevieve picked up that week's unread paper off her desk, and grabbed a bottle of water from the mini-fridge. She sat down on the couch in the office, putting her feet up. She opened the paper, and skimmed over all the news in their small town.

Most of it wasn't really news, per say, but just what was going on. Who visited who, who had a baby, etc. Living in a town of five thousand people, give or take, had its benefits, but it also didn't have too much going on. Thankfully, the college brought in fresh new minds and culture every year, which otherwise probably wouldn't exist.

As Genevieve thumbed through the announcements page, a picture caught her eye. A knot formed in her stomach, as she looked under the picture and read the names. Daniel Jacob Kent to wed Stacey Marie Beckam. Genevieve looked back up at the picture. Stacey was beaming ear to ear, and Danny was smiling, with his arm around her. She tried to read his eyes, but the black and white photo gave nothing away. He certainly didn't look miserable.

The reality hit her. She had told him to go off and find someone his own age. She had told him there was nothing for them. She had told him she would banish him from her life forever. Why then was she so torn up about his engagement? Five months ago, she had left him standing in the garden, with no choice but to move on. So he had.

The baby in her belly kicked her hard, as if to remind her of what she needed to focus on. Even so, hot tears stung her eyes and slipped down her cheeks. She knew then, even their friendship was over, and the road of life had a separate plan for each of them. All the regrets of how things had ended stabbed at her heart.

She grabbed up the newspaper, and threw it across the room. The pages separated and the announcements page fluttered down, landing back on her lap. One last slap in the face. The baby flipped in her belly, disturbed by her overrun emotions. Genevieve wiped her cheeks, and placed her hand on her stomach.

"I'm sorry, Benny. Your mommy is being stupid and selfish."

A soft little kick responded, and she could feel the baby settle. She rubbed where she felt the kick, taking a deep breath. She closed her eyes, as she laid her head back and started to hum a lullaby. Before long, she felt herself nodding off, and opened her eyes. The sky was starting to get dark. She knew she'd better head on home.

As she stood up, she saw the open announcement's page staring up at her from the floor. She looked at Danny's smiling face, and picked up the paper. She wrinkled it into a ball, and threw it in the trash can.

On the drive home, she watched the last of the sunset and marveled at its beauty. Even with all the turmoil in her life, and all the tragedy in the world, the sky continued to bless them all with an array of stunning colors every night. It was a gift that didn't matter who the receiver was.

Genevieve appreciated instead of always lamenting the things she didn't have, or couldn't have, she need to appreciate all the things in her life that she was fortunate enough to be given. A tickle ran across her middle, and she laughed.

"I know, my little Benjamin, you're right. You, Becca and Joe are not only everything I need, but more than I deserve. I just can't wait to meet you, and kiss your tiny toes."

The last of the sun disappeared into the night, and Genevieve could see the lights shining from her house, welcoming her home.

Chapter Fifteen

"It's a boy!" The nurse announced, as she held up Benjamin Joseph Howard for everyone to see. Genevieve laid her head back on her pillow, and reached her arms out for her son. As he was placed in her arms, a deep sigh of relief escaped her. She peered down at the little person she had been getting to know over the last nine months.

"Wow, Mom, he looks just like you," Becca said laughing.

In fact, Ben did look just like Genevieve. A soft coating of reddish-gold fuzz covered his head. A pair of gray eyes squinted up at them. He squawked and arched his back.

"Can I hold my son?" Joe asked quietly, standing off to the side.

Genevieve leaned back, handing Ben to Joe. Joe's eyes lit up as he stared at his son. He gently kissed the top of the baby's head, and whispered something to Ben, too soft for anyone else to hear.

Genevieve watched her husband stroll around the room slowly, grinning down at their son. She smiled to herself in sheer joy at seeing that bond form right before her eyes. Joe bounced Ben slightly, and whispered to him.

"Okay, Dad, let us all have a turn," Becca said, teasing.

Joe turned around chuckling, then reluctantly handed the baby to Becca. He came over, and leaned in to hug Genevieve. No words needed to be spoken between them. He knew the miracle she had performed, and she knew that without him, they would not be basking in the glory of their baby boy. Or their daughter, for that matter.

Genevieve couldn't help but be amazed, as she watched Becca holding Ben. Even though Becca appeared to be old enough to be Ben's mother, there was just something so sibling about them together. A connection even parents can't understand. A connection that as an only child, she certainly had never understood. Even Joe's siblings were quite a bit older than him. Other than phone calls now and then, they weren't really close. She hoped Becca and Ben would always be close. The nurse came back into the room, rolling a clear basinet. She smiled softly at them, with an apologetic look.

"I have to take the baby to the nursery for vitals and a check over. He'll be back in fifteen, or so, minutes. Mrs. Howard, another nurse will come in to take you to your room."

After Ben had been taken to the nursery, and Genevieve whisked off to her room, Joe excused himself to go peek in the nursery. Becca followed Genevieve, and sat down in a chair next to her bed. She rested her head on her hand, which was propped up on the bed. She looked seriously at Genevieve.

"All kidding aside, Mom, that was incredible! I can't believe that's what it took to bring me into the world."

"You bet, and my labor with you was way longer. I just can't believe it's been fourteen years, since they first laid you in my arms. You're just so... so big!"

"Oh thanks, Mom! Watch out everyone, huge Becca's coming through!"

"No, not like that. So grown up and all. But you're still, and always will be, my baby girl," Genevieve said earnestly.

Becca grinned slightly, and shook her head.

"Aw, Mom, don't get sappy on me now. Keep it together!"

"Ugh, you stinker," Genevieve said, and threw a pillow at her.

Becca deftly caught it, brandishing it in the air.

"Getting old Mom, I'm too fast for you. Seriously, how old are you and Dad now?"

"Ancient. I'm thirty-six, and your Dad is fifty."

Becca wrinkled up her nose, and seemed to chew on that information for awhile. She sat quietly for so long, Genevieve forgot what they had been talking about. She started to doze off, when she heard Becca clear her throat. Genevieve opened one eye slightly, and peered over at Becca.

"Mom, I mean... I know Ben wasn't planned and all, but don't you ever worry that you, or especially Dad, won't be here when Ben grows up?" Becca asked, biting her lower lip—her eyes clouded over.

Actually, Genevieve had thought about that almost everyday since she found out she was pregnant with Ben. Then again, even young healthy parents sometimes died leaving small children.

"Oh, Bec, don't worry about it. I know we are a little older, but people have babies later in life all the time. We'll be fine. People live on average into their late 70's nowadays... a lot of times way older. We aren't going anywhere!"

Becca nodded, trying to smile, her lips wobbling at the corners. All of a sudden, Joe materialized at the door, holding a bundle of squalling, angry baby.

"Someone is hungry, I think," he chuckled, handing Ben to Genevieve.

Genevieve unhooked her nightshirt, and latched Ben on. He nursed ferociously, grunting and kicking. Becca's faced turned bright red, as she looked away quickly.

"Mom, a little warning next time, huh?" she asked, and clicked on the television for something less mortifying to watch.

"How do you think *you* made it through your first year?" Genevieve teased.

Becca's mouth fell open with surprise, and she rolled her eyes. "Mom, please..."

Later, after Ben had nursed and was slumbering away, a nurse came in to tell them visiting hours were over. Joe tried to protest, but Genevieve shooed him away.

"Honey, I need my sleep... go on. We'll still be here in the morning," she said, and kissed him good-bye.

The first night with any baby is restless and hard, and Ben was no different. The hospital had a 'no baby in the bed rule', which Genevieve tried to abide by, but by midnight with no sleep, she knew she was going to have to break it. She pulled Ben into bed to feed him, and let him stay curled up by her side when he was done. They both drifted off into dreamland a few minutes later. The next time he woke her nuzzling at her side, searching for something to eat, the sun was just coming up.

Genevieve put Ben to her breast, taking the time to just adore his sweetness. His cheeks were red and rounded, as they sucked in and out, in a quest for satiation. She stroked them, awed by their softness. His eyes stayed shut, but he grunted with satisfaction.

Finally, he pulled his head back, and broke the suction. Genevieve propped him up against her chest, and started to pat his back. He wobbled his head around, and then bent forward nuzzling her neck. A low burp rumbled up, and his head popped up with an expression of surprise. Genevieve couldn't help laughing. A laugh joined her from the door. She glanced over, to see Joe leaning against the door jam, chuckling.

"Now, that's my boy," he said with pride.

Genevieve handed him Ben, and buttoned up her shirt. Ben snuggled into Joe's chest, his tiny feet moving up and down.

Joe sat on the end of the bed.

"Doesn't get much better than this, does it?"

"No, it doesn't," Genevieve answered. She looked at the empty doorway. "Where's Becca this morning?"

"Oh, she didn't relish getting up so early, so I left her back at the house," Joe replied, sniffing the top of Ben's head.

Ben opened his mouth in a big yawn, and they both laughed.

"Hard to believe she was ever this tiny, and now she's all teenager and attitude," Genevieve said, leaning forward to wipe drool off Ben's chin.

"Yeah, but she's really something, isn't she?"

"I'm so proud if her, and the woman she's becoming," Genevieve said, with tears in her eyes. "Oh, don't mind me... hormones."

Joe bent forward and kissed her. Ben let out a noise, which sounded like a cross between a cat yowling and gas. He spit up on Joe's shirt, and then fell silent again. Genevieve and Joe's eyes met with understanding, as they burst out laughing.

"Well, that's it, honeymoon's over!" Joe exclaimed.

"Here we go again," Genevieve retorted, and wiped off Joe's shirt.

A nurse peeked her head in, and smiled.

"Everything alright in here?"

"Oh, just the usual," Joe answered.

The nurse saw the stain on his shirt, and nodded knowingly.

"By the way, Mrs. Howard, your sister is really charming," the nurse said.

"My sister?"

"Yeah, the gal that was in here with you last night. With the long brown hair? I guess, I just assumed she was your sister, since you were so close," the nurse sputtered, confused.

"Oh, my! That was my daughter, Becca," Genevieve exclaimed.

The nurse raised her eyebrows, and shook her head. "Oh I'm sorry; I would never have guessed you were old enough to have a daughter that age. I thought little Ben, there, was your first," the nurse replied. "Well, anyway, let me know if you need anything."

The nurse went out, leaving Genevieve speechless. Becca her sister? Not old enough to have a child that old? She beamed with happiness. Nothing like being complimented, after giving birth to an eight pound baby, and not having had a shower.

"Yes, you are young, gorgeous and too damn pretty, to be seen with the likes of me," Joe said, grinning. "One of the nurses thought I was your father!"

"Well, come here, old man, and snuggle with your young beautiful wife who gave you a son. You lucky dog," Genevieve teased, with a twinkle in her eye.

Joe snorted and poked her foot, but obliged by climbing up next to her. They pressed together, with their son between them, and watched television. Genevieve laid her head on Joe's shoulder, and closed her eyes. Sitting here with her son, and her husband, she knew she was the lucky one indeed. Soon, they would all be together again at home, and life could only get better.

Chapter Sixteen

Genevieve combed five-month-old Ben's wavy red hair into place, and leaned back smiling. He took the fist he was sucking on, and tried to smear it through his hair. Genevieve deftly caught it, laughing.

"No, you don't! Not until your pictures are taken, you goofy boy. My, aren't you handsome," she whispered, kissing him on the forehead. She quickly rubbed off the lip prints her lipstick had made.

Ben was such a serious baby. Becca had been funny and temperamental, whereas Ben seemed to just watch everyone all the time. His cool, gray eyes seemed to reveal an old soul, rather than a little baby.

Of course he laughed, but he seemed to reserve that just

for family, and no one else. People came up on the street to coo over him, but he would just turn his head away from them.

Joe came into the room, and rattled the car keys. Genevieve looked at her watch, realizing they were about to be late for Ben's first photo session. They had waited to get his pictures done until now, because he simply did not like strangers before. She scooped Ben up, and smoothed his hair one more time.

"Okay, okay, I know. He's ready now," Genevieve said, as she brushed past Joe with Ben in tow.

Joe placed a quick kiss on Ben's head as he was being whisked by, which caused a cowlick to pop up in Ben's otherwise smoothed hair. Genevieve shot a glare at Joe, as she tried to run to the car, and smooth the cowlick down at the same time. Joe chuckled and shrugged.

"Sorry hon, but how do I resist that beautiful red head like yours?" he asked. He ducked as she threw the balled up tissue at him, which she had wiped Ben's drooly chin with.

"Becca!" Genevieve hollered back at the house, after buckling Ben in. She lifted her eyebrows at Joe, who gave her an innocent look.

"Don't look at me. I have never understood teenaged girls," he confessed.

"Neither do I, and I was one once... a very long time ago," Genevieve replied.

Becca came running out of the house, with an exasperated look. She plopped down in the seat next to Ben, and started to baby talk with him. Genevieve looked back, just as Becca was about to ruffle Ben's hair.

"Don't you dare," she warned.

"Gosh, Mom, lighten up. He's a baby, not a mannequin!"

"For the next twenty, or so, minutes he is a mannequin. These pictures are costing me an arm and a leg, and I'm not about to have him looking like a street urchin," Genevieve hissed.

Becca made a face at Genevieve, but didn't move to touch Ben's hair again. Instead, she made goofy faces, which made Ben squeal in delight.

By the time they arrived at the photographer's studio, Ben had managed to slime his hair, spit up on his vest, and lose his bow tie. All of which seemed to have Becca in hysterics. Genevieve sighed, and unbuckled Ben.

"Oh, I give up! He looks better without the bowtie... and at least the spit up is ivory like his vest."

"That's the spirit, hon," Joe teased. "Now, we are officially late, so we better just get him in there before he does any more damage."

Genevieve walked up to the counter, with Ben on her hip. The girl behind the counter smiled, and asked their name.

"Howard, and we are a little late," Genevieve said apologetically.

"No problem, the couple ahead of you ran long. Wedding pictures, ones from the wedding day apparently weren't good enough... 'too natural'. Bride wanted all of them reposed inside the studio. Boy, is she a pain in the... well, anyway, it will be about ten minutes," the girl said, waving her towards the waiting room.

Genevieve sat down, hearing the couple, or rather, the bride arguing with the photographer. She really did sound like a piece of work. Genevieve felt for the groom, who as she could tell was silent. She looked over at Joe, who put his pointer finger in his mouth like a fish hook. Genevieve busted out laughing.

A good half an hour later, the couple was finally done,

and Genevieve peeked at Ben. He was sleeping in the crook of Joe's arm, drool running down his chin. His outfit was wrinkled and wet. She sighed and rubbed her temples.

"Mr. and Mrs. Howard, we can get Ben set up in the other studio room. John, the photographer, will be in with you in just a minute," the girl said, clipboard in hand.

"Wait a second," Genevieve said, picking up Ben and starting to strip off his clothes. "Since his outfit looks horrible now, these pictures will have to be in his birthday suit."

The girl nodded, setting her clipboard down as she came to help Genevieve. Ben opened one eye, and grunted at them. Just to be on the safe side, Genevieve decided to leave his diaper on.

"I am so sorry, Mrs. Howard; we will give you twenty percent off your pictures. John is really good. He will make Ben look just as cute as can be," the girl assured, as she set Ben's messy clothes on the counter.

The cool air of the studio seemed to perk Ben right up, and he opened his eyes, peering around. As soon as the girl looked at him though, he turned his head away. The difficult couple was coming out of the studio, the bride complaining the whole way. Genevieve watched them come out, and knew she recognized the fully wedding-day-dressed bride from somewhere.

The groom came out behind his irate wife, with his head down. Ben had shifted in Genevieve's arms to see what all the commotion was about. The bride looked at Ben with disgust. She moved away from him, as if he was going to explode on her. When she moved, Genevieve caught sight of the groom, who was staring straight at her. Her heart dropped, as their eyes met.

"Oh, no way," Genevieve muttered, shaking her head. *Did it never end?*

"Hello, Genevieve. Um, how are you?" Danny asked sheepishly.

Suddenly, Genevieve knew why she had recognized the bride. It was Stacey, Danny's girlfriend, from the garden.

"I'm fine, and you? Have you met my husband, Joe?" Genevieve said, avoiding eye contact with Danny.

Danny reached out and shook Joe's hand.

"And this is my daughter, Becca," Genevieve mumbled, motioning to Becca.

Becca peered up from her teen magazine, and waved a hand. A flicker of interest showed in her eyes, until she realized Danny was with his wife. She looked back down and the magazine, ignoring them for the rest of the time.

"And who are you holding? He looks like mini-you," Danny asked, laughing. He reached out and tickled Ben under the chin.

Much to Genevieve's surprise, Ben actually laughed and looked right at Danny.

"This is Ben, my son. He is five months old... getting his first pictures," Genevieve proudly replied.

At the mention of first pictures, her eyes met Danny's, and she knew they were both thinking of Emily. He smiled slightly at her, putting his attention back on Ben.

"Would you mind if I held him?" Danny asked quietly.

"Ew, Danny, not in your suit! Why would you want to hold that baby in your suit?" Stacey exclaimed, from Danny's side.

"Because he is cute, and Genevieve is my friend. Remember my mentor from college?" Danny explained, and took Ben out of Genevieve's arms.

Ben started to gum Danny's tie.

"Oh, I remember her alright. Ugh, look, Danny, he is just ruining your tie!"

Danny ignored Stacey's outburst, and bounced Ben in

his arms. Ben seemed to dig Danny, and patted Danny's face with a wet hand. Stacey cringed in disgust. As if to add insult to injury, as Danny bounced Ben the baby bent over and puked down Stacey's dress. She shrieked and clawed at her dress, as if acid had been poured on her. Becca let out a snicker from the corner, pretending not to see the daggers Stacey was throwing with her eyes.

Joe swooped in and took Ben, as Danny tried to settle his wife. "Hey there, Bec, come help your dad get Ben cleaned up and into the studio. I think he has done enough damage here," he said, staring uneasily at Stacey.

Stacey continued to wipe her dress, and complain to herself. She glared at Danny.

"I am going to the bathroom, to get this putrid mess out of my *very* expensive dress. I trust you will be done baby holding when I get back," she spat, and stormed out of the room.

Danny and Genevieve found themselves alone in the room, but avoided looking at each other for a minute. Finally, Genevieve glanced up at him, and he met her gaze.

"Danny, what the hell were you thinking? She is horrible!"

"I was *thinking* it was time for me to settle down, and have a family and… well… so, I did."

"Just like that, and with her? Come on, Danny, you could have done better!"

"I did do better, at least in my heart, and look where it got me. Stacey and I were dating, and she can be really nice. Seriously. Plus, we are going to have a little Ben of our own soon. I'm really thrilled about that!"

"You have *got* to be kidding me. *She* is going to have a baby? She doesn't even like being in the same room as one!"

"Maybe, it will be different with her own child. Damn,

Genevieve, you of all people lecturing me on my life?" he said, averting his eyes.

"I know, but I still care about you. You are my friend. I can still want what's best for you, right?"

"You know what's best for me, and I can't have that. So let it be. I'm going to be a father, and that's something I wouldn't trade for the world. You are my friend, Gen, so support me, okay?"

Genevieve stared at her feet, as she felt tears welling up in her eyes. She wanted to support Danny, but knew he was making a big mistake. Because of her, he had jumped at the first relationship that had taken him away from her. Now, he was going to have a child with that she-witch, and probably spend the rest of his life regretting marrying her.

"Danny, I love you, and I support *you,* but I can't support something I feel will tear you apart in the end."

"Tear me apart," Danny laughed bitterly. "Been there, done that. What's the difference?"

"A lifetime... two, if you include your child. Then you'll be fighting your way out for the both of you—and it's an uphill fight."

"Look Gen," Danny said, grabbing her hand. "I appreciate your concern, but I'm a big boy. I can't say where life will take me, but I have already had to fight for two, and if I have to I can do it again."

"Okay," Genevieve acquiesced. "Remember, I'm here if you need me. Look me up anytime. And I want to meet that baby of yours when he, or she, comes along. 'Cause even if it is only half of your genetics, it will be one incredible kid!"

Danny leaned in and kissed her cheek. He let go of her hand, and walked towards the door. At the door he turned around, their eyes locking one more time. Volumes of unspoken words passed between them.

He touched two fingers to his eyebrow in a small wave, then headed out to his wife, and the life Genevieve had insisted he have without her.

Chapter Seventeen

By the time Ben was three years old, he was a regular at the nursery. Genevieve could see his flaming red hair zooming down the aisles of plants, and hear his peals of laughter echoing through every corner. He never seemed to need other children to play with. He was just as content hiding in the plants, as he was at the playground.

That summer, Becca was seventeen, and about to head into her senior year at high school. She was working full time at the nursery. She was often seen watching Rogan, Genevieve's manager, through the corner of her eye. Rogan, who was twenty-five, didn't have the time of day for her, and other than telling her what to get done, didn't speak to her much either. Becca was drop-dead gorgeous, and had her own slew of secret admirers, but she still carried a torch for Rogan, which had been lit when she was thirteen years old.

The nursery had grown so much, over the years since Genevieve started it, that she had a team of managers and workers who pretty much ran everything. She was only needed to do the paperwork, and oversee the business side, but this didn't stop her from getting her hands in the dirt everyday. She didn't think that would ever change.

As for Joe, he talked more and more about retirement. The construction business had been good to them. They had enough money saved to be able to live a fairly comfortable life without him needing to work. Like Genevieve, though, he just couldn't seem to give it up. Genevieve secretly wished he would at least slow down, because he was starting to feel a lot more aches and pains day by day.

She was thinking about just that, when Becca approached her at the nursery one Friday evening. Becca had been undecided about college, and what she wanted to do after school, so Genevieve had a feeling Becca wanted to talk to her about that.

"Hey, Mom, about done here?"

"Yup, Bec, just doing the paperwork for the week. Where's Ben?"

"He's out there, clinging to Rogan's legs and squealing. That's the one person Rogan will pay any attention to," she said wistfully.

Genevieve smiled sympathetically at her. "Give him a few years, and he will realize what he has been missing, honey. Did you need to talk to me about something?"

"Well, I have been giving it a lot of thought, and since I'd better get the ball rolling soon, I thought I would talk to you first," Becca replied, looking out the window at Ben swinging around on Rogan's legs. Then she plopped down on the couch in Genevieve's office.

"About?"

"College. If I wanted to go to college, is there any way you and Dad could help me pay for it? I could work here during it to pay some, too."

"Of course! Your dad and I have been saving for years. We will pay seventy-five percent. We want you to pay the rest, so you understand what it means to pay your own way. Have you thought about what you want to study?" Genevieve questioned, glimpsing up from her papers.

"No, not yet. I just know I don't want to be playing in the dirt the rest of my life!" Becca teased.

Genevieve made a face, and threw a paperclip at Becca.

"Your loss! Well, whatever you decide, Dad and I support you totally."

"Thanks Mom. I will go get Ben. Maybe if I stand right in front of Rogan, he will have to notice me, huh?" Becca snorted.

"Theoretically anyway, but remember he is a man, after all," Genevieve said, and winked.

She looked back down at her papers, and when she glanced back up Becca had left. She just didn't know what she would do without that girl.

Life was very good to all of them. She was glad she could offer to help pay for Becca's college, and her kids had never wanted for anything necessary. The nursery had been her dream, though it had far surpassed anything she had imagined. Even her thoughts of Danny had faded, although she always hoped he was doing well. When Ben was about fourteen months old, she had heard that he and Stacey had had a son, Marcus, and they had moved downstate to Lincoln.

That had been the moment she had entirely let go. She

125

knew Danny was more than thrilled with being a father, and she could think of no better man to be a father, well… except Joe. She wondered if Marcus looked like Danny or Stacey, and what kind of father Danny was. She shuddered to think about what kind of mother Stacey would be, after remembering the day in the photographer's studio. Maybe Danny was right, maybe it was different with her own child.

Genevieve slammed the book shut, and searched on her desk for her keys. She wanted to get home soon, because Becca was taking Ben to the movies. She and Joe would have the place to themselves. She felt around, and finally found them crammed into the keyhole on the desk. The work of Ben.

Becca had already left with Ben by the time she locked up. She had a few more hours until sunset, and wanted to stop by the Chinese restaurant to pick up take-out. Nothing was going to intrude on her and Joe's evening. A little tingle of excitement ran up her back. After all these years, they still had it.

The lights were on when she got home, and she could hear music coming out of the open windows. She grabbed the Chinese food out of the passenger's seat, and practically skipped up the sidewalk. Joe met her at the door, with a glass of wine and a big kiss. He had showered and put on cologne. Genevieve suddenly felt sweaty and gross next to him.

"Quick shower, and then dinner," she said breathlessly.

He put on his sad face, taking the food out of her hands.

"Five minutes, I swear!" she promised.

She rushed through the shower at lightening speed, making every attempt not to nick her legs while shaving. She grabbed a summer dress out of the closet, and pulled it over her head, while trying to brush out her long hair at the same time. Anyone walking in on her would think she looked like a cross between a one man band and a contortionist.

She flew down the stairs, just as the smell of the reheated Chinese hit her nose. Her stomach grumbled loudly. "Oh really classy, Genevieve," she muttered, and pressed her hand to her stomach.

Joe met her at the bottom of the stairs and whistled. He looked so handsome, his silver hair glinting in the light. The lines around his eyes crinkled, as he smiled, staring at her.

"Baby, how did I get so lucky? You're too beautiful," he said earnestly.

Genevieve blushed.

"Determination and persistence. Plus, you're not half bad yourself," she replied, and leaned in to kiss him.

His lips felt soft and rough at the same time. A little shiver ran down Genevieve's spine.

"Dinner?" he asked huskily.

"Yeah, we'd better now, or we may not get to," she answered, and pulled him towards the dining room.

They chatted over dinner about the children and their jobs, the whole time holding hands or pressing knees. It reminded Genevieve of when they were first married. She was glad she and Joe were starting to be able to, in some ways, find their way back to each other. They had always been together, but life often seemed to muddle the bond. Now with the children getting older, and both of them being able to hand off responsibilities at work, they seemed to be like young lovers again.

After dinner, Joe led Genevieve by the hand into the living room, and they started to dance. First to a slow song, and then a faster number, and then to another slow song. Genevieve pressed herself against Joe, as they swayed to the music. When that song ended, they sat down on the couch together and kissed.

Joe leaned back, and reached up to rub his right shoulder.

"Sorry, my shoulder's been acting up all day. Think I worked myself too hard, at the site today."

"Joe, you need to stop doing that! You have to take care of yourself! That's why you have employees."

"Oh, honey, I know. I promise, tomorrow I will hand more of the duties off. We were just short handed today and well, you know." He grinned at her sheepishly.

"I know. Here, sit down on the floor in front of me, and I will rub your shoulder," Genevieve said softly.

Joe obliged and rested his back against her legs. She started to knead her fingers in his shoulder, and he sighed and closed his eyes.

"Ah, magic fingers."

"You have no idea... wait until later," Genevieve said, and bent down to kiss his ear.

"Hmmm, sounds like a plan," Joe laughed.

"Joe, Becca told me today she wants to go to college for sure. She wanted to make sure we could help her out financially."

"Did she really? Wow, our little girl really is growing up. Of course, you told her we could help her, right?"

"No, I told her she would have to live out of a cardboard box, and make Tiki dolls out of her hair to sell," Genevieve said, teasing. "Yes, I told her we would pay seventy-five percent."

"Sounds good. Can you believe it? Ben starts preschool this year, Becca's planning on college next year. We have done well. I need to tell both of them how proud I am of them, and how much I love them," Joe said in a far-off voice.

"Oh Joe, they know. You always show them that."

"But I need to say it to them, so they never doubt it," Joe whispered.

Genevieve leaned down, and wrapped her arms around Joe's chest. He reached up, and wrapped his arms around hers.

"Darling, I love you. I don't deserve how good you are to me," he said quietly.

"Oh, Joe, I love you too, and I'm the one who doesn't deserve you," she said, resting her head on his shoulder. "Does your shoulder feel any better?"

"A little, it just aches something fierce, maybe I should put the heating pad on it?" he asked, rubbing his arm.

"That's a good idea, let me run upstairs and get it," Genevieve said, and hopped off the couch. Joe smiled gratefully up at her.

She was upstairs rooting under the bed for the heating pad, when she heard the crash. She ran downstairs, and saw Joe lying on the floor. He was clutching his right arm. He appeared to be unconscious.

"Joe! Joe! My God! Can you hear me?" she yelled, shaking him.

He didn't respond, so she grabbed the phone and dialed 911. When the dispatcher came on the line, she started to cry.

"Please send an ambulance! My husband's collapsed! He was saying his shoulder was hurting. I went to get a heating pad, and when I came back he was laying on the floor. Hurry please... please!"

The dispatcher told her to stay on the line, and tell him everything that had happened. Joe didn't move at all. In minutes, the EMTs arrived and rushed to Joe's side. Genevieve tried to push between them, to get to Joe, but they gently held her off, as she screamed his name over and over again.   They started CPR, and other life-saving techniques, but all their failed attempts told Genevieve what she had sensed, as soon as she saw Joe laying on the floor.

He was gone.   Her husband, her friend, her lover of eighteen years, the father of her children, was gone from their lives forever.

Chapter Eighteen

People say the stupidest things to someone who has just lost a loved one. At least, that's how it seemed to Genevieve, after Joe died. While she was busy trying to decide the best way to bury her husband, neighbors and friends constantly tried to console her, with clichés and religious ideals.

"He's in a better place," they would say.

Try telling his children that Daddy is better off without them, Genevieve would think bitterly.

"God had a plan," they would say.

A plan to rip a family apart, and leave them broken hearted? Genevieve wondered.

"God only picks the best," they would assure her.

So, what's that leave the rest of us, the scum of the earth? Genevieve fumed.

"It was his time," they said, patting her on the hand like a small child.

His time to drop dead in the living room? His time to unexpectedly have a heart attack? His time to leave his children wondering what the hell happened? His time to leave me all alone, to face every morning without him, to wake up without him, and every night to lay in torment? Genevieve cried out silently.

"He is free from the stress and pain of this Earth," they whispered.

Well, that one is probably true, Genevieve assented, *but what about me?*

Luckily, shortly after the funeral, most of those enlightened souls sunk back into the woodwork, and avoided Genevieve at all costs. Then she wasn't sure which was worse, their trite assurances, or being left to grieve alone.

She was mad too. Mad at God, for teasing her with the chance to get to re-know her husband, only to tear him away from her. Mad at couples she saw who still had each other. Mad at women she heard in the grocery store and on television, complaining about their husbands. Especially mad at herself, for not always giving her all to Joe.

Grief has a way of putting people on a pedestal, and Joe was on one of the highest. As she built Joe up in her mind, she tore herself down.

Why had she even looked at another man? Why had she gone off to college and to start her own business, when it took time away from Joe? Why had she ever raised her voice to him in anger, or grumbled about him behind his back?

These weren't reasonable thoughts, but Genevieve was

not at the point to be reasonable yet. She was too stuck in her own guilt and anger. She couldn't blame anyone for Joe's death, so she blamed herself for whatever she could.

Outwardly, she showed a composed facade, while inside she felt like she was losing her mind. When she'd hear the front door open, she'd jump up at first, thinking it was Joe. When she was making dinner, she would start to make his favorite meals. When the phone would ring, she would wonder if he was calling from work. Half the time she was screaming inside over his absence, and the other half her mind would forget he was even gone.

The nursery was being run by the staff, and Genevieve couldn't even bear to show her face there. Joe had only been gone three weeks. She just wasn't ready to figure out how to resume a normal life. Her husband of eighteen years was suddenly gone, and she didn't know how to live life without him. Some days she kicked walls and screamed at God, or cried until she felt sick.

Becca stayed out of the house, as much as possible. She worked long hours at the nursery, then drove to the state park until closing most days. Genevieve tried to talk to her, but Becca, like her mother, wasn't one to break down and let it all out easily. Genevieve knew she had to give her time, which was fine because her own grief took up most of her energy.

Then there was Ben. If Joe's death alone didn't drive her insane, Ben's grief just might drive her over the edge. Every night he would stand by the front door, waiting for Joe to come home. When Joe didn't, Ben would curl up by the door and just cry, and cry. Genevieve tried everything in her power to try and console him, but Ben's three-year-old's grief just couldn't be comforted.

One day, Genevieve found Ben carrying around a picture of Joe, which he had taken out of the photo album.

133

In it, Joe was laughing and opening a Christmas present. It seemed to be the only thing which gave Ben any comfort. Genevieve took it one night while Ben was sleeping, and laminated it. She slipped it back beside Ben's pillow, so he wouldn't even notice she had taken it.

Oh and his nightmares! Every night Ben would wake up screaming, but it wasn't like he was awake. His eyes would be open, but glazed over, and he would just scream. Genevieve was at her wits end. To be honest, Ben's nightmares terrified her.

About a month after Joe died, Genevieve heard a knock at the door. She groaned and dragged herself off the couch, where she had seemed to take up permanent residence. She peeked out, to see a little old lady standing there, holding a plate. She recognized the lady as one of the regulars from the nursery. Mrs. Shea, or something like that. She reluctantly opened the door, and put on her best fake smile.

"Mrs. Shea, right? Can I help you?"

"No, but I can help you, dear. May I come in?" Mrs. Shea asked, as if it wasn't a question.

Genevieve looked back at the state of her house, and decided it was presentable enough. She nodded and opened the door wider. Mrs. Shea made her way in, and set the plate down at the dining room table. She turned around, smiling at Genevieve.

"Please call me Birdie. I made us some shortbread, to have with tea," she said matter-of-factly.

Genevieve took the hint, and put the kettle on for tea. While the kettle was heating, the ladies sat down at the table and sized each other up. Although she had talked to Birdie here and there at the nursery, she wasn't sure how that carried over to this visit.

"Mrs. Shea... er, um, Birdie, thank you for the cookies. If you don't mind my asking, what made you come all the way over here to visit?"

"Here's the thing, Mrs. Howard, I waited one month after your husband died to come over, because I knew that was the right amount of time."

"For what? I don't mean to be rude, but what does one month have to do with anything?" Genevieve asked sarcastically.

Birdie didn't seem shocked by Genevieve's tone.

"That's it, right there. After a month, the numbness wears off, and the real grieving begins. The gloves come off. You don't feel you have to be sugary-sweet to everyone," Birdie replied, her blue eyes glinting. "That's when you need people the most, and that's when most of them stay away."

Genevieve sat shocked for a few seconds, and the kettle went off. She jumped up to get it, while she mulled over Birdie's forthrightness. Whoever Birdie was, she just might be what Genevieve needed right now. She came back with cups of tea for the both of them, and sat down facing Birdie.

"Birdie, how do you know this?"

"Mrs. Howard, you aren't the only one who has loved and lost," Birdie answered softly, as she placed a hand over Genevieve's. "Everyone has their burdens. I have buried a husband, and two children, in my time. I know the *ins* and *outs* of grief."

Unexpectedly, Genevieve let her tears flow, as they sat there. Birdie didn't turn away in discomfort, or try to make Genevieve feel better. She just let her cry. When Genevieve felt she could talk, she opened up to Birdie about her loneliness, her despair over her children's grief, her fear of a future alone, and her guilt about not always being the perfect wife. Birdie chuckled and tapped her hand.

"There is no such thing as the perfect wife, or the perfect mother, or the perfect anything. Let that go."

"I'm trying, but it just seems like when I think I have conquered that beast, it creeps in," Genevieve sniffed.

"Especially at night, right? Or when your children cry for their daddy? Or when you least expect it. That's only natural, but keep reminding yourself that you are a good wife. A bad wife wouldn't hurt so much at the death of her husband, Mrs. Howard," Birdie said, her eyes never leaving Genevieve's face.

"Birdie, please call me Genevieve. You don't know how much your visit has helped me. No one else ever comes by, or is ever honest. I feel like I'm trying to keep things together, with ever unraveling strings."

"Accept that as part of grief. Let grief happen in its own time, and its own way. As for your son and his nightmares, they are called night terrors. He is just venting his grief, in his own way. When he has them, don't try to talk to him, just lay him down and soothe him. He won't even remember them. He has to work things out in his own time, too."

"But it hurts so much to see him suffering. I want to take away his pain," Genevieve cried.

Birdie nodded her head, touching her hand to her heart.

"I know you do, but you can't. His grief, and your daughter's, are theirs to work through—you can't change that. Just love them, be there, and don't be afraid to let them know you are hurting too."

"Birdie, I hope you don't mind if I ask, but how did you lose you husband and children?" Genevieve asked.

"Well, our first baby died at age two, from cancer. Back then, there was nothing they could do. We were told to take her home, and make her comfortable... to let her die," Birdie choked up, and touched her hand to her nose.

"That's was the hardest one to bear."

Genevieve reached out and took Birdie's hand, as a fresh wave of tears came over her. Birdie's eyes were focused in another time and place.

"After Lola's death, I thought I could never face another one. It took me years to get it together, and rejoin life. But I knew I had to, for our son Micah's sake. Then, I lost my husband Harold, when he was about the same age as your Joe. That was over thirty years ago. I guess I was in my forties then, and Micah was on his own—in the Army."

"How old are you now, Birdie?"

"I am seventy-seven. Micah was killed in action in Vietnam, shortly after Harold's death. I once had a family, then I just didn't. No one to cook for, no one to have holidays with. Just me," Birdie said sadly.

"Oh, Birdie, how did you cope? How are you not angry at God?"

"Oh trust me, I was! I had a few choice words for God, but then I realized I was just lashing out in pain. It was no one's fault. It is just the way life is. A few years later, though, I was blessed again. I came to understand, that whether we want it or not, life always has more in store for us," Birdie said, and took a sip of her tea.

Genevieve mulled over what she had just heard, even though she knew it would take more time for her to get to that place... if ever.

The day quickly passed, and Birdie readied herself to leave. She gathered up her things to head for her car. Genevieve followed her, hugging her at the door. Birdie chuckled, and hugged her back.

"Birdie, I hope you will come and visit again," Genevieve said earnestly.

"How about if we get together for tea and cookies, every Thursday afternoon?" Birdie suggested, titling her head slightly.

"It's a date!" Genevieve exclaimed, and both women laughed. Genevieve realized how weird it felt to laugh again.

Birdie said her good-byes, and headed out the door. Genevieve watched the remarkable woman she just met, shuffle down the path. For the first time since Joe died, there was something other than heaviness in her heart.

She thought it just might be hope.

Chapter Nineteen

Genevieve wished she could say after Birdie's first visit she was healed. The one thing she had learned for sure, over the year since Joe had died, is one never totally heals from a loss of that magnitude. A scab forms and moments of peace and normality slip in, but in an instant an event, a feeling, a memory comes in and shears the scab away—leaving the wound exposed all over again.

The sun still rises every day, and no matter what, open wound or otherwise, life goes on with the expectation to take one along—willing or not.

Birdie had kept her promise, and met with Genevieve weekly for tea. She also convinced Genevieve to join a widow's support group at the hospital. Genevieve was reluctant to attend, fearing she would be surrounded by gray-haired old ladies, who wouldn't understand her. She was surprised to find out she wasn't even the youngest widow of the group!

That honor, or misfortune as it was, went to Dehlia, a twenty-five year old mother of one. Dehlia's husband apparently had had a taste for booze and fast cars, which he stupidly mixed one night, and killed himself. This left Dehlia, and their two-month old son, Roderick, to pick up the pieces of their shattered life. Dehlia was incredibly strong, and often had insightful words of advice for the older ladies of the group, Genevieve included.

Dehlia and Genevieve quickly became friends. Becca started to watch, now sixteen-month-old Roderick, while they attended meetings. Roderick seemed to bring out an interest in Ben, who would chase Roderick around the house. They loved to jump in mounds of pillow they had piled in the living room, or cuddle up to watch cartoons.

Ben was doing better in the year since he lost his father. He no longer stood at the door every night crying, waiting for Joe; although, when headlights would pull in the driveway, a look of hope would cross his face, which made Genevieve's heart break. The picture he had carried of Joe had now moved into a frame beside Ben's bed, and laughter had found its voice inside him again. His night terrors continued nightly, but Genevieve learned to just quietly comfort him back to sleep.

Genevieve had her moments. Grief is not a forward moving action all the time. Sometimes it is a roller coaster, with its ups and downs. Some mornings she got up, drank her coffee and went to work, without realizing the pain of Joe's absence. Other times, she lay in bed and cried for hours, her eyes closed, hoping to wake up from the nightmare. It was one step forward, and two steps back some days.

Often she felt like she was running in place.

Becca had graduated from high school, and was anxiously awaiting the start of college in the fall. Genevieve had convinced her to stay home to live, at least for the first year, especially for Ben's sake. Becca had agreed, and even seemed relieved at the idea. After all they had been through, it seemed none of them were ready to let go of each other. Becca offered to continue on at the nursery throughout her college years, though Genevieve had a sneaking suspicion that had more to do with Rogan, than the family.

For the year anniversary of Joe's passing, Genevieve decided to have a luncheon at her house for the widow's group, seeing as how they had practically pulled her through the last year. She knew it would be hard to face people on that day, but she decided that going into the second year of grief she was going to face the pain head on—instead of always running from it.

Becca had graciously offered to take Ben with her for the day, more so because she didn't want to have to hear about death anymore.

Genevieve gave out the invitations at the next meeting, and explained what the occasion was. A few women balked at the idea, but others looked at her with a knowing she could not get elsewhere. Everyone agreed though, whatever she needed to do for herself was okay.

The week leading up to Joe's death was horrific. Genevieve kept having dreams in which she had forgotten to pick him up somewhere, and she would be driving around and around, lost in a big city searching for him. Every time, she would wake up shaking, and not be able to sleep for hours. She couldn't even fathom if it was this bad, how horrible the anniversary of his passing would be.

She tried to stay as busy as possible, and keep her mind occupied.

The day before the luncheon, Becca, Ben, and Genevieve planted a Redbud tree outside the living room window, in memory of Joe. Ben seemed so stoic, as he threw small handfuls of dirt in the hole. He kept running around, talking about Daddy's tree. Genevieve knew they were making an important step in remembering Joe. They had all come to accept he was gone, but they were learning they could still carry his memory with them through their lives. When they were done planting the tree, each child picked up a statue they had chosen, to put near it. Genevieve also placed a statue of a bear near the tree.

"I picked this one out, because Joe, your daddy, was always like a big teddy bear to me. Protective and warm, and maybe just a little fuzzy," she said, laughing through her tears.

Becca smiled, and wiped a tear from her eyes. She set down a statue of lion next to the bear.

"Well, I picked this lion out, because Dad was always so strong and handsome. And even when he was mad and roaring at me, I knew it was because he loved me so fiercely," she whispered, and let the tears roll unabashed down her face.

Genevieve took her hand, and they both looked at Ben, who was clutching a superhero statue tightly to his chest.

"Daddy's my hero, and can fly now," he said, and leaned down to put his statue by the tree.

Then to their surprise, he leaned and kissed each one of the statues, and the tree saying 'I love you, Daddy' after each kiss. Then he turned, and took Becca's hand.

"Time to go in now," he stated, and led her to the door.

Genevieve stayed behind, and stared at the tree. She took a leaf, and rubbed it between her fingers.

"I love you, Joe. I'm sorry if I ever failed you. I'm sorry if I ever let you down. I'm sorry if I ever made you angry or disappointed you. You were, and always will be, my friend and my husband, and I will never ever forget you."

A feeling of warmth passed over her. She bent down to draw a small heart in the dirt. She knew, even though Joe's death would always leave a hole in their lives, it didn't mean that she couldn't go on.

Words that Birdie had said to her, on one of her first visits, echoed in her head.

"Just because his life ended, doesn't mean yours has to."

The day of the anniversary of Joe's death started like any other. Genevieve noticed how the weather was just the same as it had been, that fateful day the previous year. Becca and Ben were exceptionally quiet, so she decided it was best to let them talk about their feelings only if they wanted to. Neither did. As Genevieve was drinking her coffee, the phone rang.

"Hello?"

"Genevieve, it's Birdie. How are you dear?"

"Oh you know, muddling through. You are coming today right? Please say yes, I need you here," Genevieve begged.

"Well, that's why I was calling. I have to go the eye doctor this morning, and he is dilating my eyes for my exam. I can't drive, but my nephew, DJ, offered to drive me. Is that okay?"

"Oh, of course, Birdie, and he is more than welcome to stay as well... the more the *miserier*," Genevieve said, in an attempt at humor.

"Okay, then we will be there a little early, to help you set up. I may be half blind until the medicine wears off, but I am anyway," Birdie said cheerfully. "Until then, dear."

Genevieve hung up, and looked around the house. It was a mess! At least that would keep her mind busy until the luncheon, and then that would keep her busy until the evening. The evening would be the real challenge, followed by the night...

Becca came flying down the stairs, and thrust a package into Genevieve's lap. Genevieve stared up in surprise. Becca impatiently motioned her to open it.

"Now, don't make a fuss, Mom, it's just something I saw, and thought of you," she said lightly.

Genevieve tore open the wrapping paper, and caught her breath. Inside was a ring with Joe's, Ben's, Becca's and her birthstones embedded in it. She peered up tearfully at Becca, who was blushing.

"It's a family ring. I thought it was fitting. It even has a place you can add stones—if you ever needed too."

"Oh Becca, it's beautiful, and so perfect. Thank you, my baby girl," Genevieve cried, from her heart.

Becca bent down, kissing her on the cheek, and disappeared as fast as she had come. That was Becca, though, not one to stay around for emotional moments.

Genevieve had gifts for Ben and Becca too. She had found pictures of each of them with Joe, and had put them in key chains. She had placed them in Becca's car on each seat, so they would find them when they went out. She wanted them to know their daddy was always with them.

Becca and Ben left shortly after, to go to paddle-boating at Chadron State Park. Genevieve heard Becca honk before they left. She glanced out to see both of them smiling, holding up their key chains in the window of the car. She blew them a kiss, and they drove away.

She started making sandwiches for lunch, and turned the crock-pot of soup on. She found herself to be incredibly nervous, as this was the first time since well before Joe's death she had entertained. She hoped conversation would carry itself along, and there would be enough food. Dehlia called to say she couldn't make it, because Roderick had the flu. Genevieve was disappointed, because Dehlia and Birdie were the ones she felt most comfortable with in the group.

About an hour before guests were supposed to arrive, she heard a knock at the door. Birdie stood there with dark sunglasses on, feeling around for the door jam. Genevieve couldn't help but laugh, taking Birdie's hand.

"Birdie, you really didn't have to come early. I could knock over tables and chairs all by myself... thank you!"

"Oh, you!" Birdie exclaimed, and slapped at Genevieve—missing her by a mile.

Both women giggled, and headed inside the house.

"My nephew is grabbing a few things from the car for me; he'll be in a minute. Oh, and he brought his son. I hope you don't mind."

"Not at all, I just wish Ben was here. How old is his son?" Genevieve asked, leading Birdie to a chair.

"Three or so. Little thing, but full of spunk! I think he fell asleep in the car on the way over," Birdie replied, feeling around the table for a cup.

Genevieve poured a glass of lemonade, and placed it in Birdie's searching hand. Birdie smiled, and took a sip.

"Thank you, dear, now what can I do?"

"Birdie, you can just sit there looking gorgeous. I will go help your nephew carry in your things. I'll be right back."

Genevieve slipped on her sandals, and started for the door. She flung the door open, and rushed out—right into Birdie's nephew, who was carrying his sleepy son in. She stepped back and started to apologize, when she stopped short. She couldn't believe her eyes! Danny was standing in front of her, with Marcus in his arms. Danny set Marcus down, who ran right in to Birdie's arms, and stepped forward. He wrapped his arms around Genevieve, hugging her tight.

"I am so sorry, Gen, about Joe. I just got back in town myself, and Birdie was telling me about her friend, Genevieve, who lost her husband. I was so surprised," he murmured into her hair.

Genevieve laid her head against his chest, and the tears began to flow. Why was it Danny seemed to open a door in her, which so many people walked right by?

"Danny," she said, and stood back to look at him. "You are Birdie's nephew? But she said her nephew was called DJ."

"My initials, she's always called me by them. Don't you remember, I told you I had a non-blood great aunt who took me in, when I was a kid? That's Birdie!" he said, smiling in Birdie's direction.

Genevieve stared hard at Danny, and couldn't believe how good he looked. Her mouth opened to say something, but she found she was at a loss for words.

He gazed back at her, and winked.

"So, shall we go in, or just stand here letting the flies in all day?"

Chapter Twenty

As other guests arrived for the luncheon, Genevieve busied herself at a furious pace. She was trying to not focus on either of the two noticeable events of the day. The first was Joe's absence, the second—Danny's not unwelcome presence.

She found a comfort in her old friend, and admittedly, the lonely part of her appreciated any physical contact she could get. Eighteen years of constant physical closeness with another human being, was not easy becoming accustomed to the lack of.

Except for Danny and Marcus, everyone attending the luncheon was a woman; Genevieve hoped Danny didn't feel out of place. She glanced out of the corner of her eye, to check on where he was, and if he was in need of rescuing. In fact, he was not. He was chatting amicably with Louise, an older widow from the group, and a friend of Birdie's. Then Genevieve understood, he probably knew most of these women better than she did, since he was Birdie's great-nephew.

Suddenly, she noticed Danny spotting her staring at him. He grinned at her, and raised one eyebrow. She blushed, glancing away, giving her attention to a bag of rolls she was trying to untie. At best, this luncheon was going to be awkward, and at worst it would be a catastrophe, she feared.

Neither was true. Everyone seemed at ease, and many of the ladies gave Genevieve a card, or a hug and knowing look. They had all already been through the first, and sometimes second or fifteenth, year without their husbands, and appreciated where Genevieve was at. Some were remarried even, but still attended the meetings. *'Once a widow always a widow'*, Genevieve had heard them say often.

Marcus was not even a bit shy, as he ran around charming everyone. He definitely looked like his mother, with her dark hair and green eyes. He had Danny's longer nose and wide smile, though. Genevieve hoped Ben would be home before Danny left, so he could meet Marcus. She thought they would get along well.

"Do you need any help?" a low voice asked, from behind her.

Genevieve turned, and peered up at Danny.

"With this stuff, or mentally?" she asked, sticking her tongue out and rolling her eyes.

Danny laughed genuinely, and started cleaning up plates off the table.

"Well, Gen, I learned a long time ago you can't be

helped mentally, so I guess it's this stuff I'll help you with." Danny narrowly missed the plastic spoon thrown at his head.

"Do you give your wife this much crap?" Genevieve teased.

A shadow fell over Danny's face, his smile vanishing. He peeked at Marcus with a panicked expression, then took Genevieve's arm, guiding her to the back porch.

"Um, Gen. Stacey left," he whispered, staring at his feet.

"You got a divorce? Oh I'm so sorry," Genevieve stammered.

Danny shook his head.

"I wish it were that simple. Stacey left me and Marcus. Just left, never came back. She sent the divorce papers in the mail, and gave me full custody of Marcus."

"Oh, my God! Poor Marcus. How can a mother just do that? And you... oh, Danny, she was crazy to give up you and Marcus," Genevieve said, her hand grasping his arm.

"I guess we weren't what she wanted, after all. I thought having Marcus would make everything better, but instead it drove her away. Marcus doesn't understand... he is real torn up about it."

"They hide it so well, don't they? I would never have known. Ben is still dealing with Joe's death, not too well, I might add. I was hoping he could meet Marcus, if Becca brought him back in time."

"Damn, Gen, I'm sorry, this isn't about me today. You lost your husband—here I am rambling on about my divorce," he apologized.

He placed his hand over hers, and their eyes met. Genevieve could see little lines around his eyes—his face looked thinner. Although some was from age, she could tell a lot was from stress. She leaned her head on his shoulder.

"We make quite the pair, don't we?" she murmured, and laughed.

He leaned his head on hers, nodding.

"Heckle and Jeckle?"

"Nah, more like Tweedle Dee and Tweedle Dum," he replied, laughter shaking his body.

"Well I'm not the Dum! I will be the Dee," she said, poking him in the ribs.

"Okay, Dee, that makes me Dum."

Marcus came tearing into the porch, with an expression of terror on his face. As soon as he saw Danny, he ran up and wrapped his arms around Danny's legs. Tears streamed down his cheek.

"Thought you left, Daddy. Was scared," he sobbed.

Danny scooped him up, and kissed him on the cheek.

"Little man, I will never leave you."

Genevieve slipped out, leaving Danny to comfort his small son, and made her way back out to the luncheon. Birdie and Louise were talking about a quilt show in town, later on that afternoon. Other ladies were getting their things ready to go, and came to say their good-byes to Genevieve. She thanked each one of them as they left; soon she was sitting there with Louise and Birdie.

"Genevieve, you didn't tell me you knew my nephew DJ. He is such a sweet boy... my blessing," Birdie said, patting Genevieve's hand.

"Yes, I didn't know he was called DJ, though. I always called him Danny. I was his mentor in college, and we became friends," Genevieve explained.

"Not to mention, I mowed her lawn once," Danny said, as he sat down at the table, with Marcus still in tow.

Marcus climbed down, and ran over to climb in Birdie's lap.

"You did? Well, that must have been years ago, DJ! Oh, and Genevieve, I am the only one who called him DJ. He needed a fresh start when he came to live with me, and I wanted him to know that he was something special and unique to me. So, I called him that, and it just stuck," Birdie said, slipping Marcus a piece of cookie.

"It's such a small world, you being Danny's great-aunt. He told me about the aunt who took him in as a child, but I never knew when I met you, Birdie, that it was you! And I haven't seen Danny since the time we ran into him, and Stacey, in the photo studio," Genevieve replied, glimpsing at Danny.

Their eyes locked in remembrance, and understanding. Danny slightly nodded at Genevieve, as if to say, *you were right*. She turned down her mouth for just a second, because she didn't want to be right. He kept her gaze, shrugging.

"Well, it is remarkable, but I don't believe there are any coincidences in life. Both you and Danny, and your children, have suffered great losses. Maybe you needed to find each other again, now," Birdie said, smiling at both of them.

Genevieve could see in Birdie's eyes, she knew Danny and Genevieve had a deeper connection than most people.

The front door flew open; Ben came rushing in, dragging Becca behind him. Becca appeared exhausted, ready to collapse. Ben stopped in his tracks, searching the room for Genevieve. When his eyes landed on her, he ran up and wrapped his small arms around her.

"Mom, the park was so much fun! We saw ducks, fish, and even a snake! Becca got me candy and hotdogs!" he exclaimed, his eyes big with excitement. He peered around at everyone, but his eyes stopped on Marcus. "You wanna play?"

"Sure," Marcus said shyly.

Genevieve could not believe the change in Ben. He was usually reserved, but something about the day, and Marcus, brought him out of his shell. Marcus hopped off of Birdie's lap, and followed Ben upstairs to his room. Genevieve and Becca exchanged expressions of sheer astonishment.

"Wear you out did he, Becca?" Genevieve asked, chuckling.

"Honestly, Mom, I don't know how you do it!" Becca replied, and sat down next to Birdie.

She snagged a cookie off a plate, and shoved the whole thing in her mouth. She glanced around, her eyes resting on Danny.

"Oh, Becca, how rude of me. Do you remember Danny? You met him a few years ago, when we were getting Ben's picture," Genevieve said.

"Oh yeah, the one with the wife who Ben puked on. I remember," Becca said, sizing Danny up. "How's she doing?"

Danny shifted uncomfortably in his chair. Stacey was obviously not a subject he wanted to discuss. Genevieve felt for him, and at the moment really hated Stacey for what she had done. She looked over at Becca, who was apparently waiting for an answer.

"Let's just say, she's no longer in the picture," Genevieve replied, kicking Becca under the table, giving her the eye.

Becca's eyebrows rose, and then she nodded.

"Sounds good, she was kinda uptight anyway," Becca said simply.

"You have that right," Birdie chimed in.

Danny looked as if he wished the conversation would drop, and Birdie took the cue.

"So, DJ, if you don't mind, Louise and I are planning to

head over to the quilt show. She can take me home from there. If you're okay, driving home without me."

"Aunt Bridget, I think I can manage. After all, I have driven for at least a few years," Danny kidded.

Genevieve hadn't realized Birdie was short for Bridget. Everything was falling neatly into place.

"I'll stay and help Gen clean up, while the boys are playing. How's that sound?" Danny offered.

"Great!" Birdie and Genevieve replied, in unison. They stared at each other, snickering.

Birdie and Louise headed out shortly after, as Becca searched for a tent in the basement. She, and few of her girl friends, were going camping that night at the state park. Genevieve knew it was best to let Becca deal with things in her own time and way. Danny collected up all the dirty dishes, while Genevieve put the food away. They worked in silence, as they often had back at the greenhouse.

Becca came up with the tent and kissed Genevieve on the cheek, before she headed out the door. She hollered something up to Ben and left. Genevieve heard her car start up and pull out of the drive. Upstairs the boys were thumping and laughing. Genevieve hadn't seen Ben so happy in so long. She knew this visit would do a world of good for both boys.

Once Genevieve was done, she stopped to look out the kitchen window. The sun was just starting to set, and the sky was a shade of light lavender. An overwhelming sadness crept in, as she was back to the realization that just one year ago she and Joe were planning a night alone, and within a few hours she was standing in this kitchen—alone for life.

Danny cleared his throat, and she turned to see him standing on the other side of the kitchen. She looked at him standing there, like lighthouse waiting for a lost ship.

She tried to make her tears stop, and put on her brave face, like she had for everyone for the past year. Her eyes stung and her chin quivered. One solitary tear escaped and ran down her cheek.

Danny crossed the room and stood in front of her, with pain in his eyes. He gently reached out and wiped the tear from her chin with his thumb. Somehow, being comforted made more tears slip out, and Genevieve gave up trying to fight them. Danny enveloped her in his arms, and just held her. She sobbed into his chest, soaking his shirt.

The whole year of trying to be strong and be there for everyone else, came crashing down around Genevieve, as she let someone else take care of her.

It only seemed fitting that person would be Danny.

Chapter Twenty-One

Life is not a movie, which wraps up at the end of the story, and fills in all the confusing pieces by the end. Often the wrongs outweigh the rights, the idea of normal doesn't exist. There are less *shoulds,* and more *coulds.* All driven by the needs of the human spirit. At the end of a good life, one hopes to just have made the world a better place.

Genevieve felt this, when she was with Danny. She knew she should send him home, and go back to being the grieving widow. But her heart wanted to talk to him, to share the pain of the past year. To hear how he had dealt with his divorce, and his son's grief. She wanted to connect to another human being, who could hold her and wipe her tears.

So when Danny took her hand, and led her out of the kitchen to the couch, she went willingly. She was tired of running away to do the right thing. She wanted to do the needed thing, which was to lean on her friend in her time of need. Danny sat down on the couch, pulling her down towards him. She sat and leaned her head against his arm.

"Now, why don't we start at the beginning, Gen? What's been going on inside of you this last year?" he coaxed. His arm was around her back, and he rubbed her shoulder with his thumb.

"Well, you know, since Joe died last year, I have been just trying to keep it together. The kids..."

"Not about the kids, about you. I know you well enough, baby, to know you put yourself aside to fix everyone else, and I'm not having it. I want you to talk about you," Danny said, taking her hand in his own.

A deep sigh let out of her, as she closed her eyes. As if a gate was unlocked inside, her voice poured out of her.

"Danny, last year I thought I had the world in my hands. A son, a daughter, a loving husband, two thriving businesses... everything a person can dream of. Then Joe died. In my grief, I grasped his death brought to light more, than just my needing him. It also brought to light the fact I accept no matter what comes my way.

"I'm a passenger in my own life! I went to college and that was me, but even then, I only did what wouldn't interfere with my family and their needs. When Joe died, I tried to focus on the kids, but they didn't want me... not like the way I wanted them to. So, all of a sudden, I was face to face with me, and all the running and denial I have done for years," Genevieve explained, and paused to catch her breath.

Danny sat silent, taking in all she had to say, and not trying to lead her thoughts in any direction.

"Without Joe, I have been so damn alone! Not just on the outside, but on the inside. I didn't know how much I had given over to the idea of wife and mother, until at least one of those roles was ripped away from me. Then I was bared naked, with only a shell of who I was destined to be.

"I am lost, and my heart aches with loneliness. I don't even know where to begin to find me again. And it's not *me* the mom, or the business woman, or the friend. But *me,* who is all I have left, when everything else falls away. When I lost Joe, I lost not only my husband, but who I thought I was for the last eighteen years," Genevieve said, as fresh tears slipped down her cheeks.

As she spoke, the trueness of her words shocked even her. She had never told anyone, maybe even herself, these things. Somehow, with Danny it was natural and cleansing.

"Genevieve, I don't have those answers, because I have spent my life wondering where the hell I fit, in this world. Except that year with you, in the greenhouse, I have constantly been stumbling through, just getting by emotionally," Danny confided.

Genevieve turned with surprise, to meet Danny's gaze. She couldn't believe he understood where she was coming from.

"Danny, you are always so together. How could you feel lost?"

"You look together, too, Gen... doesn't make it true does it? Sometimes, I still feel like that ten-year-old kid who knocked on your door, all those years ago. I was searching then, and I'm searching now. I made the mistake of thinking Stacey could help me find myself. She was so in control—I figured she knew what life was all about. She was just as lost.

"The only good thing I got from her was Marcus. I'm trying my best to give him whatever it takes, so he doesn't feel like I do. Before I had Marcus, there was only one time in my life where I didn't feel like I was out floating in space, with nothing to grip on to," Danny sighed.

"When we were together at the greenhouse," Genevieve finished for him.

His eyes widened in surprise and he nodded, pulling her back to lean on him.

"I know, Danny, I feel the same. Maybe we keep running from something that is meant to find us."

Danny was about to say something, when the boys came running down the stairs all excited. They tore into the room, chattering at the same time. Genevieve held up her hand, and laughed.

"One at a time guys, I can't understand you!"

"Mom, Marcus and I have decided we are brothers now," Ben said excitedly.

"How do you figure that?" Genevieve asked, confused.

"Because my mommy left... and Ben's daddy left. So we are like brothers," Marcus chimed in.

Genevieve and Danny exchanged a glance and shrugged.

"I guess in a way you are. Brothers in life's lessons," Genevieve acquiesced.

The boys grinned at each other, and ran back out of the room, as quick as they had come.

Genevieve turned to Danny. "I hope it was okay I said that. I couldn't see the harm."

"No, I think it's what both of them need right now. They can understand each other, better than the rest of us probably can. Give them what they need, no harm," Danny said. He looked at his watch, which Genevieve saw was the one she had given him for his graduation. It was after nine, and the boys were still playing hard.

"Would you like a cup of coffee?" she offered.

Danny kissed her knuckles, and nodded.

"Let me help you."

Back in the kitchen, under the bright lights, Genevieve took the chance to admire Danny. His attention was focused on measuring out the coffee. He was still tall and lean, but his blond, curly hair had darkened slightly from a white-gold, to the color of ripe wheat. She resisted the urge to run her hands through the curls. The back of his neck was tanned, and his back was taut with muscles. As if he could feel her eyes on him he peered expectantly.

"What's up, Gen?"

"I was just looking at you, to see if you have changed at all. You have, but in good ways... well except the dark circles under your eyes. Those I understand," Genevieve replied, unembarrassed.

Danny watched her, and came to stand closer. He reached out, running a finger down a strand of her hair.

"You haven't changed much either. You are still stunning," he said, in all seriousness.

Genevieve blushed from head to toe.

"Stop, I'm forty years old... I have changed a lot."

"So, you're forty. That doesn't make you any less beautiful, or desirable. From the moment I laid eyes on you, as a child, you took my breath away. Forty is just a number. You are who you are. And *you* are beautiful. Your hair is the color of amber, and your eyes are a captivating gray, with specks of green dancing in them," he whispered, bending closer. He brushed her cheek with his fingers. "You're skin is like newly churned butter... your body is like that of a goddess."

Genevieve sucked in her breath, when his hand went around her waist. She instinctively put her hand on his shoulder, as her other hand went to the back of his neck. She pulled him closer, and their lips met. He placed his hand on her back, pressing her to him. His lips, warm and smooth, held hers in suspense. She tightened her fingers around his curls, and ran her tongue over his lips. His mouth opened slightly, his tongue delicately touching hers. A fire ran through her body, and she gasped.

Danny pulled away, staring into her eyes, his own burning with desire. She returned his gaze, and he cupped her chin in his hand. He leaned down and kissed her lightly on the lips, just as the tea kettle went off. They both jumped back, laughing shyly. Danny let his breath out, and grabbed the kettle off the burner.

Genevieve's hands trembled, as she took the top off the French press and poured the coffee in. Danny brought the kettle over, and poured the water slowly in. Genevieve watched his long sinewy fingers, imagining what it would feel like to have him run them over her body. A shudder passed through her, and she shook her head to clear it.

She went over to take sugar and cream out of the cupboard, and set them shakily on the counter. Danny came up behind, and wrapped his arms around her. She sighed, resting back against him. He chuckled quietly, and kissed the top of her head.

"Not much changes there, does it, Gen? I can't be near you... without wanting you in every way," he murmured into her hair.

She turned around, and memories of the last day at the greenhouse flooded her mind. If he had known how badly she had wanted him then, how badly she wanted him now. She turned her face up, and kissed him softly on the lips.

"I know, Danny, I have always known that feeling," she said honestly. "As much as you have ever wanted me, I have wanted you."

Danny's ears turned pink and he took the sugar and cream off the counter. He came across like a little boy, who was just told a dirty joke for the first time. Genevieve couldn't help but giggle. He turned even pinker, and stared straight at her.

"Really?"

"Really, you have no idea," Genevieve replied, unabashed.

She handed him a coffee mug, and poured herself a cup of coffee; the steam rising up, twirling and dipping in the air. He followed suit, silently peering at her from the corner of his eyes.

"Come on, let's have our coffee before we get ourselves in trouble here," Genevieve giggled.

They went back to the living room, and sat down with their coffee. They made small talk and listened to the boys, who were starting to peter out from the sounds of it. Genevieve found out Danny had quit his job at the state park, when Stacey had wanted to move out of town. Instead, he had worked in an office. He had been miserable, but his dressing up everyday for work made Stacey happy. For the time being. Nothing made her happy very long. One day she had just headed to work, and never came home. After a panicked search, thinking something had happened to her, Danny found out she had simply moved out.

Danny had moved back to town with Marcus, after the divorce was finalized, because he wanted Marcus to have some family other than himself. Birdie was delighted to have her boys back. She let Danny rent a small guesthouse on her property. Marcus loved living there, and it was the only thing that had gotten him to stop asking where Mommy was.

It had been five months since Stacey had walked out, three since the divorce was finalized. Danny was hired back on at the park, while Birdie watched Marcus during the day.

Genevieve told Danny about Becca and her plans for the future. She told him about how Ben had been coping the last year, and how Phil, a guy from Joe's work, was already hitting on her. She suspected he was more interested in Joe's share of the construction business, but either way she was disgusted by him. Genevieve thought she saw a flash of jealousy in Danny's eyes, when she mentioned Phil, but it was gone as quick as it had come.

"I don't even want the share of the construction business, and am more than willing to sell it, but Phil just irks me so bad! I'd rather sell it to someone else for half the price. I just wish he would leave me alone... he's like a vulture," Genevieve confessed.

"I'm sorry you have that to deal with, too. Some people just don't have any compassion," Danny replied. "I could take him out, if you wanted me too."

Genevieve actually giggled at this, and shook her head no, although she knew Danny wasn't serious. He flexed a muscle in his arm, raising his eyebrows comically. They both laughed hysterically. It felt so good to just let it all go, to have fun.

They fell silent, and listened out for the boys. No sound came from the room, so Danny motioned to go upstairs and check on them. They crept up the stairs, and peeked in Ben's room. The boys were asleep on Ben's bed. Ben on his side, with Marcus lying over his feet. Both boys had an action figure in one hand, and Marcus had his thumb in his mouth. Danny and Genevieve smiled at each other, carefully slipping out of the room.

Once they were back downstairs, Danny glanced at his watch. It was after eleven.

"Well, I guess I should get Marcus and head home," he said quietly.

Genevieve looked intently at him, taking his hand.

"Please don't think me forward, and I'm not saying we should do anything, but I really don't want to be alone tonight. I have slept in the bed for a year by myself, and tonight I just really want you to stay beside me. Please don't go," she whispered, and clutched his hand.

Danny looked surprised, and then his eyes softened. He squeezed her hand.

"Are you sure, baby? I mean, we won't do anything, I can just hold you. Are you really sure?" he asked sincerely.

"I am sure, Danny. I need you tonight," she said, as she led him to the bedroom.

Chapter Twenty-Two

In the bedroom, Danny and Genevieve looked at each other shyly. Although neither of them intended to do more than comfort each other, and sleep, having come into the bedroom together was a step neither one had imagined would ever come to pass. Genevieve pulled a silk nightgown out of her top dresser drawer, and Danny politely turned away, while she put it on. Even having him in the room while she changed made her blood hot. She turned around and stared at his back, which was tense with the moment. She cleared her throat softly.

Danny turned, and looked at Genevieve standing in her nightgown. It was far from frumpy, even though it was one of the most covering ones she owned. She felt her breath come faster, and wished she could hide under the covers. Instead, she walked over and unbuttoned Danny's shirt. She slipped it from his shoulders, peering at his lean contoured stomach. Her hands rested on his tight shoulders, and he glimpsed at her sheepishly.

Genevieve ran her fingers down his chest and over his waist. He was just so beautifully made, long and golden. His blue eyes met hers, as he placed his hand over her fingers, stopping them in their tracks.

"Stop that, or we won't stop," he said huskily.

She nodded, and a small smile of acceptance touched the sides of her lips. He reciprocated the smile, and they stood there reveling in each other's presence... in the possibilities of the future. Danny led her to the bed, and they sat down together. Although this was the bed she and Joe had shared for so many years, Genevieve had moved the bedroom furniture downstairs. This way, she at least didn't feel trapped in the memories of lost times since Joe's death.

Genevieve knew Danny was exercising great restraint in not wanting more, because she felt it herself. He rested back on the bed, and motioned for her to lie down next to him. She crawled up and into his arms. She laid her head on his bare chest, letting out a sigh of pent up stress she didn't know was in her. Danny rubbed her arm with one hand, and rested the other one behind his head.

True to their word, they did not cross the line. All night they lay together, cuddled, but their clothes stayed on. That's not to say they resisted all urges. Genevieve breathed in the smell of him, and a ripple of excitement tickled her belly. For the first time in a long time, she was not alone. Not to mention, with someone she had felt pulled to for many years. She gazed up at him, and he bent down to kiss her. Genevieve pressed herself up to get closer to him, and found herself lying on his chest, with his hand on the small of her back. They lay like this and kissed for some time, not wanting to open their eyes and remember where they were. For this night it was just them against the world, them only for each other.

Eventually, exhaustion won out and they drifted off to sleep. Genevieve woke a few times in the night, and pressed herself as close as she could to Danny. He would turn and wrap his arms around her in sleep. For the first time in a year, Genevieve felt safe and wanted.

The light of morning came in quietly, waking Genevieve up too early. She yawned, and peeked at Danny. His eyes were closed, his blond eyelashes like little curled feathers. She thought he looked like a prince lying there. His mouth was closed, but relaxed in sleep. Genevieve reached out and ran a finger down his long, straight nose. One of his eyes opened slightly, peering at her, and he grinned.

"Good morning, baby, sleep well?" he asked, and opened both eyes, as he propped himself up on one of his elbows. He rested his other hand on her waist.

"Better than I have in a long time. Thank you for staying," she replied.

Her fingers traced the scar on his right arm. Every time she saw it a bolt of pain pierced her heart. After all, that was a mark of the time they first met. A price he paid to meet her. Danny watched her face as she looked at the scar. He read her pain, and moved his arm to take her hand.

"Gen, I would suffer that, and more, to be with you. There is nothing I wouldn't face, to be by your side," he said sincerely.

Genevieve stared at him, amazed at his honesty.

"I don't want you to ever be hurt for me. Ever. I love you too much."

166

"You love me?" Danny asked, his voice tinged with surprise.

Genevieve recognized what she had said, and contemplated it. *Yes, she did love him.* Not just as a friend, but more. She peeked at him and nodded. Danny's eyes were round, reminding her of the boy who had paid a huge price to be near her.

"Oh, baby, you have no idea what that means to me. I have loved you so long. There was a time, I thought that would be my burden to take through life," he said, kissing her fingers. "I love you."

Genevieve was speechless with the power of what had been revealed. She sat up, and pushed her hair out of her face. In a moment like this, it was easy to forget the roadblocks. She was over twelve years older than him. She was a mother and a widow. She had so much baggage. For goodness sake, she had stretch marks! Danny might be caught up in the moment, but in time he would see her as an old woman. His eyes would probably be turned by a younger woman. Yes, she loved him. Enough not to want him to feel trapped. He sat up next to her, and took her by the shoulders, as if he had read her mind.

"Gen, I love you. Pure and simple. I don't care about our ages, or our histories. I love you. It's enough," he said earnestly.

He was about to go on, when they heard the front door open. Genevieve's face went pale with panic.

"Becca," she whispered, and bolted out of bed.

She grabbed her robe, and threw it on. Danny stood up, and put his shirt back on.

"Oh, what will we tell the kids?" Genevieve cried softly.

"We'll tell them we love each other, Gen, this is not the end of the world," he said, begging her with his eyes to remember their night.

Genevieve was too upset, and ran a nervous hand through her hair.

"Mom, you up?" Becca called, as she headed down the hall towards Genevieve's room.

Genevieve felt like a high school girl, about to be caught by her mom, making out with her boyfriend. As Becca looked in the room, and saw Danny and Genevieve standing there in their bedraggled clothes, her face took on an expression of utter shock.

"Mom, what the hell is going on here?" Becca screamed, throwing open the door.

Genevieve and Danny stood frozen, trying to think of how to explain. Becca turned on her heel, and stormed back down the hall. Genevieve ran after her, catching up with her at the base of the stairs.

"Becca, wait. It's not how it looks. We didn't do anything, he just stayed to keep me company," she tried to explain.

Becca glared at her, and started up the stairs.

"Oh, Mother, grow up!"

Danny came in behind Genevieve, putting his hands on her shoulders. Becca disappeared around the bend, and Genevieve turned to face Danny. Looking at him she knew she was willing to fight for him, but she didn't know how.

"Um, why don't you go and get some coffee down at the doughnut shop. I'll try to smooth things over here," she said gently, and leaned up to kiss him on the cheek.

He nodded, and slipped his shoes on.

"You'll be alright?"

"I'll be alright, Danny, just give me some time to explain to her. Do you need money?"

"No, I'll get it. I'll pick up some doughnuts for the kids, too. Is Marcus okay to stay here?" he asked, grabbing his keys.

Genevieve nodded. She grasped his hand, and walked outside with him.

"I'm sorry, Danny, she's just adjusting. I'm sure seeing her mother in the arms of a younger man is not high on her list of wants," Genevieve explained, once they were out side.

"I can understand that," Danny said, and bent down to kiss her.

She pressed in to his warmth, letting him hold her, before she had to face her daughter's wrath. Their lips were just separating, when she heard someone yelling behind them. They whirled around to see a very irate Phil Sloan, the guy from Joe's construction company, standing there red-faced, with flowers in his hand.

"What the hell do you think you are doing?" he stammered, glaring from Danny to Genevieve, then back to Danny again.

He threw the flowers on the ground, and crossed his arms. Genevieve couldn't figure out what he was doing at her house, and why he was so angry.

"Phil, why are you here?"

"I came to see you. I thought we could go have breakfast, but I see you already have a new young piece of meat to satisfy your needs," Phil spat.

Danny visibly tensed, and his jaw set in a firm line.

"Excuse me, Phil," Genevieve said strongly. "I did not invite you here, and you have nothing to say about who I have at my house. I think you need to leave."

Phil's eyes got huge, and a wave of fury crossed his face. He took a step towards Genevieve. In a flash Danny was standing in front of her. Phil took a swing at Danny, grazing his cheek. Danny flew at him, and had him around the throat.

"We don't know each other well enough, for you to

even *think* you should be doing that. Got it, Phil?" Danny said, through clenched teeth.

Phil visibly shrank back, and his pupils dilated. He put his hands up backing away, once Danny let go of his throat. He quickly made his way down the sidewalk towards his car. Once he was a safe distance away from Danny, he turned around to glare back at them.

"That's okay, I don't want none of any cradle-robbing whore!" he yelled with venom, and hopped in his car.

Danny made a move to go after him, but Genevieve grabbed his arm, dragging him back in the house. Danny's breath was coming in short rasps; Genevieve had never seen him so angry. She slammed the door shut once they were inside, and turned to look at him.

Becca was standing at the bottom of the stairs, her eyes wide with amazement, and her mouth hanging open. Apparently, she had seen everything that had just transpired.

"Upstairs! And keep the boys up there," Genevieve ordered.

Becca could tell her mom was serious, and ran back up the stairs.

Genevieve gently took Danny's chin in her hand, turning him to face her. His cheek was scratched where Phil's gaudy diamond ring had caught it. She reached up to touch it, but Danny grabbed her hand, and met her gaze fiercely. She pulled her hand away, and touched his cheek. His eyes softened, and he rested his head on hers.

"Damn it, Danny. Let me put something on that, before that scum of a man's germs infect you."

She took him by the arms, and sat him at the dining room table. He slouched in the chair, wincing when she rubbed alcohol on the scratch. His eyes were distant, making her understand maybe that was how he dealt with the abuse in his parent's home. Tears stung her eyes, and she knelt down, laying her head on his lap. He put his hand on her head, stroking her hair.

Genevieve knew as long as they tried to be together, the world would be against them. Because she was a widow, because he was so much younger, because he wasn't Joe, because apparently she didn't deserve to be happy. She lifted her head up, and peered in to Danny's eyes. She couldn't bear for him to be hurt for her again.

"Danny, we can't do this. The world will be against us... and you will keep paying the price for loving me," she whispered.

"I don't care about that, Gen. When I said I would do anything to be with you, I meant it. I will do anything," he said, determined.

"But I can't stand by and watch you get torn apart for me. I love you too much for that. It's just not our time right now."

"When will it be then, Gen? When everyone who ever knew us goes away? That will never happen! I love you now! I need you now! How long are you going to make me wait?" he said, tears welling up in his eyes.

Genevieve laid her head back down on his legs, and cried.

"I don't know, my Danny, I just don't know."

Chapter Twenty-Three

Danny's eyes never left Genevieve's face, while he was loading Marcus in his truck. Neither one of them knew how to leave things, but Genevieve had some unfinished business to deal with, before she could think straight. Danny climbed in his truck, and sat staring at her for a minute, before starting it up. The expression on his face tore Genevieve apart. In her own way, she was causing his pain, in trying to save him from it.

He nodded slightly at her, and pulled out of the driveway. Marcus waved exuberantly, grinning. Genevieve smiled at him, and raised her hand in a wave. Then they were down the road and gone. She sighed, and turned to go back in to the house.

Becca was sitting at the table with Ben, eating cereal. She looked up at Genevieve, with an apology in her eyes. She had settled quickly, after her outburst in seeing Genevieve with Danny. No apology needed. Genevieve felt for her daughter, whose whole world was changing faster then she could probably get her bearing. Genevieve leaned down and kissed the top of Ben's head, and then Becca's. Becca visibly relaxed.

"I'm sorry Mom, I was being stupid. Danny is nice, and if he makes you happy, then I'm okay with it," she said truthfully.

Genevieve smiled wearily. Even though Becca was okay with everything, Genevieve still felt she was at the bottom of the hill looking up. She just didn't know if the climb would ever end, and she couldn't see putting Danny through all that misery.

"Thanks, Bec, but I don't think Danny and I will be more than friends... just too much to deal with."

Becca frowned and faced Genevieve head on.

"Mom, you give up too easy! Fight for what you want."

Genevieve appreciated Becca's candor, but at eighteen it was a lot easier to be willing to spend endless time fighting for love. She wasn't eighteen, and she wasn't sure she had that much energy left in her. She patted Becca's hand, and walked back to her room to get out of her robe and into her work clothes.

Peering at the bed, where she and Danny slept the previous night, a pain shot through her heart. It all seemed to mesh last night, and then this morning all hell broke loose. She could understand Becca's feelings, but Phil's tirade?

Her mind drifted back to when she saw Phil standing on her sidewalk infuriated, his bald head shining in the sun. How dare he? Who the hell did he think he was, just

173

showing up at her door, and questioning who she was with? New ire rose in Genevieve, and she quickly threw a pair of jeans and a tee shirt on. She knew she had to deal with that little weasel, or it would eat at her. This morning he caught her off guard, but this afternoon she would have the upper hand.

Becca and Ben were watching cartoons, when she came back out. Ben seemed so rested and content; it was at that moment she remembered he didn't have any night terrors the previous night. Marcus sleeping over had calmed Ben, and a wave of relief swept over her.

"Becca, can you watch Ben for a bit? I have an errand I have to run today, and it can't wait," Genevieve asked, as she pulled her hair back in a pony tail.

Becca nodded and waved, barely looking up from the cartoons. Genevieve smiled inwardly at her two children, many years difference in age, but both entranced at some inane cartoon character splitting his pants on the screen. She shook her head, chuckling as she headed out the door.

Driving across town, she thought about how she would handle the situation. She could almost feel Joe pushing her to deal with life, and stand up on her own two feet. As she pulled too quickly into the construction site parking lot, a few startled workers turned and glanced in her direction. One of them recognized her, shaking his hammer in the air to wave at her. She waved back and smiled. She parked in Joe's old spot, and jumped out of the car. A few whistles floated in her direction. She glared over with her best disapproving look. She was greeted with an even louder whistle. She made eye contact with the whistler, who turned slightly red.

"I'm looking for Phil Sloan, where is he?" she asked forcefully.

Taken by surprise, the whistler pointed over towards the

foremen's shack. He watched her walk away, his eyes never leaving her behind.

Genevieve took a deep breath, and threw open the door of the shack. Sam, Joe's buddy and partner, glanced up in shock. When he saw it was Genevieve, he leaned back in his chair grinning, and waved her in. The little weasel, Phil, was standing on the other side of the shack. He stared over at her in contempt.

She didn't know why Joe and Sam had brought him on board with the construction company. He was lazy, shifty, and had more than once tried to convince Joe into retirement. Joe hadn't budged, so Phil had jumped on his chance for Joe's shares, almost before Joe was in the ground.

Genevieve waved seriously at Sam, and marched directly over to Phil. He puffed up his chest, like he was going to set her straight. She almost wished she could have taken a picture of his expression, when she raised her hand and slapped him as hard as she could across the face. He started to raise his fist in response, but stopped when he saw Sam get out of his chair.

"How dare you show your scummy little face at my house uninvited, and call me a whore?" she fumed.

She could hear a few breaths suck in, out of astonishment, around the shack. She was sure no one knew of his intentions and visits to her. He looked around and saw everyone's mouths hanging open. She turned back to Phil.

"I don't want you. I will not give you Joe's part in this company, and you'd better keep your slimy ass away from me and my family," she seethed.

She could tell Phil wanted to blow, but knew he would be hung out to dry if he dared attack Joe's widow in front of everyone. His fists were clenched at his sides, and his greasy nose shined with sweat of held-in fury. Genevieve's handprint was appearing on his face. His thin mustache quivered above the line of his set mouth. Genevieve knew if they were alone, he would most likely knock her to the ground. Phil had always had a hot temper, and this about pushed him to the edge.

Sam stepped over, placing his hand on Genevieve's shoulder. She instinctively stepped back towards him, feeling his chest against her back.

"I don't know what has been going on, but Genevieve, know that Joe and I created this company alone. His part of it is yours to do with what you want. Phil will not be coming around anymore," he said firmly, never taking his eyes off of Phil's face.

Genevieve knew Sam was true to his word, and his friendship to her and Joe was solid. She nodded and thanked him. Sam stood there for a minute, and then the phone rang. He stepped away to answer it.

Phil snarled at her.

"Better tell your little boyfriend to watch his back," he said, under his breath.

Genevieve laughed out loud.

"Please, Phil, after this morning you'd better be glad you still have a windpipe, because you were about two seconds away from having it ripped out," she said forcefully, pointing her finger at his neck.

He swallowed hard.

"This isn't over, chickie," he snorted.

"Oh, you have no idea how over this is. Because if you come near me, or my family, ever again, I will personally kick your ass," Genevieve said, glaring at him.

He tried to hide his surprise, but made no sound as she turned on her heel and walked out. Suddenly, Genevieve felt like, with or without Joe, she would be able to take on

176

the world.

She got in her car, and turned up the radio. She started to drive out of the parking lot, when she saw Sam standing at the door smiling at her. She touched two of her fingers to her eyebrow and waved. He nodded with appreciation, waving back at her. She sped out of the site, and headed for Birdie's house.

Birdie was in a house dress when she opened the door, her hair in curlers. She looked at Genevieve standing there, and beamed.

"I wasn't expecting you, but then again I guess you owe me one on that," Birdie chuckled, referring to the first time she stopped by Genevieve's, after Joe's death.

She opened the door to let Genevieve in, and led her back to the kitchen. Birdie's house reminded Genevieve of her grandma's, and she felt a tidal wave of calmness wash over her. She sat down at the table, glimpsing around.

A young picture of Danny hung on the wall. He must have been about fourteen years old when it was taken. His eyes held a lifetime of pain then; they actually held less now. Birdie poured her a cup of tea, and sat down across from her.

"Okay, out with it," Birdie said directly.

Genevieve knew there was no sense in lying, or hiding anything from Birdie, so the whole story poured out, from the moment she met Danny to the current afternoon. Birdie listened quietly and took it all in. If she was shocked by Genevieve's confession, she didn't show it. When Genevieve stopped talking, Birdie tilted back in her chair, thinking about what she had heard. She leaned forward, and took Genevieve's hand.

"Do you love Danny?" she asked, point blank.

Genevieve nodded, and smiled weakly.

"Yes, Birdie, I really do, but dragging him down with

me hardly seems fair."

"Well, fair is all relative anyway. Not much in anyone's life is truly fair. Danny is a grown man, not a boy, and he knows what he is doing. How to take care of himself," Birdie replied sincerely.

"But, Birdie, I'm afraid if he is with me, it will never end. The disapproval, the whispers, the anger. I don't want him to be hurt for me," Genevieve confided, laying her head down on her arms.

"I don't want him to hurt either, Genevieve, but don't you think by not letting him love you, you are hurting him?" Birdie asked, touching Genevieve's hand.

Genevieve sighed. She knew what Birdie was saying was true, because she had told herself the same thing, but she was afraid to let it determine anything. She looked up at Birdie through red-eyes.

"Birdie, I am so much older than him, that society will never accept it. They will never take us seriously. Just me as a cradle-robber, and him as a disillusioned little boy," Genevieve said.

Birdie bobbed her head, chuckling.

"How much older than you was Joe?" she asked.

"Fourteen years older."

"And how much older than Danny are you?"

"Twelve... almost thirteen years," Genevieve answered. She knew where Birdie was going with this. "But, Birdie, it's different when the man is older. People accept that; even applaud the man for it. With women, we are perceived as immature and dirty, and our younger men are considered nothing more than boy-toys."

Birdie considered this, and shook her head. "Well then, Genevieve, you and Danny are fighters... prove them wrong."

"I guess I just have to think about everything. I can't

make a decision now. I don't want to screw everything up by jumping to any conclusions. Danny deserves more than that," Genevieve said, and took a sip of tea. It felt warm and soothing going down.

Birdie watched her, with sadness in her eyes.

"Just remember, Genevieve, life is short. Don't wait to long on things you want, lest they disappear."

Genevieve finished her tea, and thanked Birdie for the advice. She knew she had to head home before it got too late. Becca had a shift at the nursery; she needed to get back in time for her to leave. She kissed Birdie on the cheek before she headed out.

As she was driving out the long driveway, she saw Danny's truck coming in. She knew she had to talk to him, so she slowed and pulled off to the side. He stopped as well, and climbed out of his truck. They met in the center, between the two vehicles. In Danny's eyes was a question only Genevieve could answer. She walked up, and wrapped her arms around his waist. She buried her face in his dusty shirt, hugging him as tightly as she could. He ran his fingers up and down her spine, resting his chin on the top of her head. They stood in the middle of the drive, knowing what was coming, but not wanting to face it. Finally, Genevieve pulled back and stroked his scratched cheek.

"Just give me time, Danny. I need to figure out who I am, before I take someone else on this tumultuous ride with me," she said honestly.

He winced, but nodded.

"I have waited this long, I will wait forever for you," he said, wrapping his arms back around her.

She only hoped he really knew how long it could be, or that she didn't lose what she loved, before she could even grab hold of it.

Chapter Twenty-Four

In her journey of self-discovery, Genevieve found a power within herself she never knew she had. She also found reason to use it. Phil Sloan had spread terrible rumors about her around town. Often while she was out shopping in the grocery store, she would hear snickers and whispers behind her.

She did her best to ignore them. One time, though, when she heard a couple of women her age, loudly criticizing her from another isle, she threw a couple of eggs over the shelves at them. They couldn't see her or her them, but from their shrieks and following silence, she knew she had made her point.

Becca went off to college. She seemed to have a

definite skill in business administration. Like Joe, she had a knack for numbers and multi-tasking. That was the part of running the nursery Genevieve despised most of all, so she let Becca manage the books. Genevieve went back to playing in the dirt, so to speak, and never felt more satisfied at the end of each day.

Ben and Marcus played together a few times a week, and at least once a week spent the night at each other's house. Dropping off and picking the boys up made Genevieve feel like a divorced parent sharing custody. If she and Danny were to run across each other, they were always polite, but distant. He respected her need for time, but eventually a gap grew between them. She fully expected him to move on one day, because she was taking too long in finding herself.

Birdie never pressed the issue, but she always made little comments about life and love, which Genevieve knew were directed at her. She loved Birdie, but couldn't explain to her, that until she opened her heart up to herself, she couldn't offer it to anyone else. She had to be able to face all her fears, and not care about what other people thought. She just wasn't quite there yet.

Danny continued on at his job at Chadron State Park. Being it was a small town; he and Genevieve saw each other often. Through Birdie, she had heard he had purchased an old ranch house outside of town, which he was renovating. Genevieve knew of the place, and had often fantasized about living out there away from everyone. She was slightly envious of Danny, but kept herself in check, knowing her choices were her own.

Ben started preschool in the fall, and at the boys' insistence, Marcus started soon after. Both boys thrived being around each other, making Genevieve glad for small miracles. Ben's night terrors had completely stopped, and he talked of Joe in a loving, but free, way. As the second year wound down without Joe, Ben worked through his grief. Now, he told people about his dad watching over him, but there was no ache behind his words—only pride.

Soon winter let go to spring, and the nursery's business picked up again. Genevieve was busier than ever, enjoying every minute of it. Becca was finishing up her finals, and still working at the nursery. One day, Genevieve caught Rogan watching Becca, from the corners of his eyes. Finally, he had noticed the beauty right in front of him. Becca was too busy with the accounts to even notice. Genevieve laughed at the irony of it all.

It had been almost a year, since Genevieve had asked Danny for more time, and she was actually coming to a place where she knew who she was and what she wanted. She had tried to make eye contact with Danny, time and again, when dropping off Marcus or passing him at the preschool, but he just kept his head down and his eyes averted. Genevieve feared she had done just what Birdie had warned her about. She had hurt him so badly, he had drawn away.

Dehlia, the young widow from the support group, had come in for a job at the nursery, out of the blue one day. Genevieve had hired her on the spot, and never regretted that decision. Dehlia's quick humor and outgoing personality brought life, to a staff of recluses at the nursery. Her son, Roderick, soon joined the boys at the preschool, although he was only in the morning class because of his age. He, like Dehlia, was always smiling and friendly. Genevieve made it a point to learn all she could from Dehlia. They spent every Friday night, going to the movies, or out to dinner, for just them. Becca would watch the boys, so the moms could have time alone. Genevieve didn't know about Dehlia, but that time reminded her of who she was, long before she had dedicated her life to everyone else.

One Friday night, as summer approached, Dehlia called and told Genevieve she couldn't go out, because she had a date! Genevieve couldn't believe it. Even though she was happy for Dehlia, her own heart ached to be wanted again. Her thoughts drifted to Danny, and the night he had stayed to comfort her. Her body ached to feel his arms around her again. She wondered if it was simply too late for them.

The following Monday, as she was dropping Ben off to school, she spotted Danny getting out of his car with Marcus. She and Ben walked every morning since they only lived a few blocks from the school, so she had to run to catch up to him. The boys saw each other and ran to one another. They started talking incessantly, leaving Danny and Genevieve standing alone. He avoided her gaze, and scuffed his sneaker on the pavement.

"How are you, Danny?"

"Just banner, how are you?" he replied coldly.

"I'm good. The boys seem to be doing well, don't you think?" she asked upbeat, trying to get him to talk.

He peered over at the boys and nodded; his mouth in a grim line.

"Yup."

"I was thinking, maybe we could get a coffee, or something," Genevieve suggested.

Danny stared at her skeptically.

"I don't know, Gen, not sure I want to jump into this again," he replied, his blues eyes glinting in the sunlight.

Genevieve took a deep breath. It was too late. The boys ran into their class, without even a look back.

"I understand… it's not fair of me. I just miss you," she whispered.

His eyes never left her face, but he remained silent.

She reached out to touch him, but he pulled away and stepped back.

"Well, I'm sorry to bother you. Talk to you later... I guess," she said softly.

He turned and walked away. As she watched his back disappearing into the distance, she wanted to run after him and scream his name, to beg him to stay, to wrap her arms around him and never let go. Instead, she stood helpless, watching the man she loved walk away. What ever happened to he would wait forever? She shook her head, and bit back the tears. Who was she to expect someone to wait forever, when she kept pushing them away? She took a deep breath, and headed for home.

After that, it was Birdie who started picking up and dropping off Marcus from Genevieve's house. The boys never went to Danny's house anymore, since he had moved out to the country. Genevieve knew it was time to let go, and to focus on what she knew she definitely had. The kids, the nursery... and herself.

One day, on a lark she went to the hair salon, and had her hair cut to right below her shoulders and layered. She had long hair for so long; it shocked her to actually see her face. The way the hair stylist did her hair, reminded her of the old forties actresses, with their hair curled forward towards their face. Genevieve decided she liked it, and the hair stylist went on and on about how much younger she looked.

Over the summer Genevieve started walking more, and one day in passing a mirror she stopped and caught her own breath. Her body hadn't looked this good, since she was twenty! She didn't appear day over thirty, even though she was forty-one. It reminded her, Danny was quickly approaching thirty. On the surface, they really didn't look so different in age. Then, why had she pushed him away so hard?

The following fall Ben started kindergarten, so he and Marcus didn't see each other as often. Marcus was in his second year of preschool. The boys only played together once a week. They still remained best friends, though, for which Genevieve was relieved. Ben's kindergarten was the other direction, but still close enough where Genevieve could walk him to school. It was her time in the morning to set her mind straight, before heading to the nursery.

One October morning, they headed out as usual for school. Although the morning was cool, Genevieve slipped on a pair of white shorts and a tank top. Thinking twice, she ran and grabbed her sweatshirt. Ben was anxiously waiting at the door, jumping up and down. Genevieve put her hair back in a ponytail, and made a face at him.

"I'm coming, I'm coming. I know you have a big day today! Field trip to the museum, right?" she asked, quickly running a brush through his hair.

Ben nodded excitedly, and ran out the door. Genevieve followed, and gasped as the cool air hit her legs. She rubbed them, and second-guessed wearing shorts. No time to change though, because Ben was halfway up the street. She pulled her sweatshirt over her head, as she ran to catch up with him. She grabbed his hand, and kissed the top of his head.

Genevieve dropped him off at the school yard, with a quick peck on the cheek. Ben was young, but still a boy, who didn't want his Mom kissing him in front of everyone. He ran off with a group of friends, leaving Genevieve standing watching him.

It was so hard to let go. He seemed so small and vulnerable on the playground. A large boy ran past Ben, almost knocking him over. Genevieve bit her lip to avoid calling out to see if he was okay. She waited until the bell rang, and all the kids ran to their classes, before heading back towards home. Ben grabbed his bag and darted towards his class, without as much as a glance back. Genevieve watched her little boy, realizing even he knew when it was time to let go.

She strolled slowly towards home, taking the time to appreciate the leaves that had started to turn. The hues of reds and gold always took her breath away. It made her sad the changing of the colors only lasted a few weeks. These mornings, she was in no rush to get home and ready for work. This morning she sensed something in the air, and decided it would be smart to move a little faster. When the first crash of lightning hit, she knew she'd better run.

She hadn't made it two blocks when the rain started, and she ran searching for some place to duck in. She saw the baseball field up ahead, and made a bee line for it. Right about the time she discovered the fences to the field were locked, marble sized hail started to pelt her. It felt as if someone was throwing rocks at her head, and the rain was freezing on her legs. Home was another quarter mile away, and the storm was coming harder and harder.

Lightning crashed above her head, which made her jump and scream. She knew it was way to close for comfort, and truly feared being struck by the next bolt that came through. She started to run as fast as she could towards home, praying every step she would make it safely. Hail stung her body leaving red marks, which would certainly become bruises within a few hours. Had she known *this* was coming, she would have driven Ben to school.

She darted out across the road, almost in front of a vehicle, when she heard the horn honking at her. She threw her hand up in apology at the driver she couldn't see. She could hear the vehicle coming up beside her, and she turned to apologize. Through her squinted eyes and the rain, she could see the driver of the truck was rolling down their window.

"I'm so sorry for running out in front of you. I got caught in the storm, and am trying to make it home," she screamed over the wind, her vision impaired by the driving rain.

"Hop in, I'll give you a ride," the driver replied, sounding somewhat familiar over the roar of the storm.

Normally, Genevieve wouldn't just get in someone's car, but it was getting scary out there, and this *was* a small town. She ran over to the passenger side, and opened the door. A wave of relief washed over her, as she peered into the bluest eyes she had ever known.

Danny smiled at her, pulling her into the truck. She slammed the door and glanced over at him, her breathing heavy from running, and her heart rapid from more than the exercise.

"Thank you, Danny. You saved me," she said earnestly.

He looked over her, and grinned.

"What do you say we take a drive, and find a place to talk?" he asked, handing her a roll of paper towels to dry off with.

She stared at him, trying to figure out what change had come over him. This was not the same Danny who had walked away from her, before the summer. He had a look of sheer grit on his face, which made a shiver run down Genevieve's spine.

"I would like nothing more than that," she said, and reached for his hand.

Chapter Twenty-Five

Danny let go of Genevieve's hand to switch gears, as they headed out of town. From the direction they were heading, Genevieve knew they were going out to the state park. Her heart thumped hard in her chest, keeping beat with the pounding rain. She wondered what would come of this ride. Danny kept his head facing forward, and the music cranked up. He gunned it outside of town, and they sped down the highway towards the park.

Genevieve dried off the best she could with the paper towels, but her sweat shirt was soaked all the way through. She was thankful she'd had the foresight to wear a tank top underneath, as she pulled off the heavy wet material. Once the sweat shirt was off and discarded on the floor, the heat of the truck warmed up her arms. She slipped off her soaking sneakers, and wiggled her toes under the floor vent to heat them up. Danny had a comb tucked in the console, so she pulled her hair out of the pony tail and started to comb through the tangled mess. At least with the layers, she could get through it.

She popped down the visor mirror to part her hair, and realized her cheeks were flushed... not from the storm. She snapped the visor back in place, and glanced over at Danny, who had remained silent. He looked back at her for a second—unreadable—and then focused back on the road. Genevieve was too afraid to reach out and touch him again, so she folded her hands on her lap, and breathed in deeply to settle her heart beat. By the time he turned into the park, her heart, and the rain outside, had slowed.

They drove past the cabins, following a road that led up to the top of the hills.

Danny stared at her for a moment, and asked hardly, "So have you figured out who you are yet?"

Genevieve jumped at the sound of his voice, and peered over. A steel glint was in his eyes—she felt like a child being reprimanded by a parent.

"Um, yes," she whispered.

He watched her, nodded, and looked back out towards the road. Nothing else was said for a few minutes, and then they drove up into a parking space pointed back towards Chadron. Genevieve had never been up here, and was caught by the beauty. Danny left the engine running to leave the heat on, and turned to face her. He reached out and turned the radio down, fixing his eyes on Genevieve's face. She felt like he was waiting for her to explain what she had come to, and started to open her mouth. He put his hand up to silence her, and she sat back against the door.

Watching him so close, she could see the year and a half

apart had changed him as well. He seemed like more of a man…. clearer of what he wanted.

She wanted to tell him she had decided she wanted him—that no one and nothing would change that, but she sensed her time to explain and make the decisions was over. A knot formed in her stomach, wondering if he was just done with her for good. He glanced out over the trees, silent. Genevieve didn't know what to do. About the time she felt she should say something, he turned and stared at her intensely, his blue eyes a mixture of emotions.

"You know, Genevieve, I have known you, really known you, for about eight years now. You have always told me how things had to be, how I should feel, what I should do. I took it, because you seemed to know what life was about, and because I knew I couldn't have you unless you came to that decision.

"I respected your marriage, because I believe in marriage. I even went out and got married, and had a family, because you thought I had to be able to do that to experience life," he said, sitting back against the door.

Genevieve wanted to apologize for all those things, but from the look in his eyes, she knew it wasn't her time to talk. He sighed and looked at his fingernails. Then his eyes rested on her again, and he went on.

"I have loved you for years, and you have continually pushed me away. Granted, you had reason at first, but then you kept doing it when you didn't have reason. You hurt me worse than anything else in this world could have. So, I started to shut down, to avoid the pain of being rejected. I would see you places, and my heart would just hurt, so I started to push those feelings away. Then you show up, and ask me to have coffee with you, as if we were still the same old friends. I couldn't be both; I couldn't have a heart, and not have one."

"Danny, I'm so sorry. I didn't mean to hurt you! I was trying to be fair, to give you a chance to see the horrendous mistake you were about to make. For goodness sake, you are closer to my daughter Becca's age! It's her you should be looking at... not me," Genevieve said unconvincingly.

Danny laughed bitterly, glaring out the window. He was silent for a minute, and Genevieve had no idea what he was thinking. His jaw clenched, and he slammed his fist against the steering wheel. Genevieve's eyes got round, and she went to touch him. He stopped her, fixing his eyes on her.

"Is that what you think, Gen? That as long as someone is closer to my age, I can love them? Damn it, Gen, I don't love Becca, I love you! You are the one I wanted to be with. You are the one who kept me up at nights. It's your face I see when I'm hurting. It's your touch I want to feel when I lay in bed at night. It's your voice which haunts me when I think I'm going to spend the rest of my life alone!" Danny yelled, in despair.

Genevieve could see all the years of pain and suffering she had caused him. It wasn't just a school-boy crush he felt for her. He genuinely loved her... and what had she done with it? Treated him like a child, who didn't know what was best for him. She ached to reach out and touch him, but he had pulled away so much she was scared to. She tentatively reached out her hand, and was surprised when he grabbed it in his own. He stared at her, with tears in his eyes.

"Don't you see nothing matters but you and me?" he asked, his voice low. "Don't you see it doesn't matter if you are older, if you have a child my age, if you think I don't know about the world, if people give us dirty looks, if you think I have no experience? It doesn't matter," his voice trailed off.

"I know it doesn't matter to you, Danny. It doesn't to

me, either, but I didn't want you to suffer, because you thought you wanted to be with me," Genevieve explained.

A flash of anger went through his face.

"*Think* I want to be with you? After all this time, Gen, I'm pretty sure I *know* I want to be with you! And suffer? I have suffered every day since I first laid eyes on you again, in the greenhouse. I felt drawn to you then, but figured it was just another crappy hand life had dealt me— you were already married.

"Then you responded to me at your house last year, and I hoped maybe destiny had brought us together again for a reason. But you pushed me away again. I don't care about the world, I care about you!" he hollered.

He opened his truck door, and got out in the rain. He slammed the door, and Genevieve could see him standing out in front of the truck, facing towards town. Rain poured down on him, but he just stood there.

Suddenly, it all made sense. This was who she was *supposed* to be with. This boy, turned man, had sought her out time and again to be close to her, and in her heart of hearts she knew that was all she wanted too. She didn't care what anyone thought. She was not going to walk away from true love again. She would just have to make him see she wanted him, and wouldn't push him away anymore.

She shoved the door open, and dashed out into the rain. She ran up behind him, and wrapped her arms around his soaked waist. He stood tense for a minute, not responding. She could feel his heart allowing the ice to melt, as his back slumped in acceptance. He turned around, and put his arms around her. All the pressure slipped away, and they stood crying, holding each other, as the rain washed away their pain.

"I promise, Danny, I am yours forever. I won't hurt you again. I swear," she cried.

He tilted her chin up to him, and she could see his eyes had softened to the old Danny's. He kissed her gently on the lips, and she melted into him. The cool rain didn't stand a chance against the heat of their bodies. He pulled away and gazed at her, with a love she hadn't seen in a very long time from anyone.

"I won't let you. The ball is in my court, and I'm calling the shots," he said firmly.

Genevieve sighed, happily handing over the decision to him. He led her back to the truck, and they climbed in. Danny pulled her towards him, and she snuggled up as close as she could to his side. She pressed her lips against his, moaning as his warm hands pressed on her back. They spent the better part of an hour exploring each other.

Catching her breath, she sat back and took his hands in her own. She rubbed her fingers across the calluses, which lined his otherwise smooth palms. His hands were tanned from working outside, and his long fingers were thin and hard from years of working in the environment. Just the sight of them made her pulse quicken. She lifted his hand and kissed his fingers. Danny just watched her in amazement. She tilted her head curious towards him, as if to ask what was surprising him.

"No one has ever loved me like you do," he said, answering her silent question. "You see me... all of me, and I have never had that."

"What do you mean? You have been married, you have been, well, you know... intimate, with Stacey," Genevieve replied, confused.

Danny's cheeks flushed, and he glanced away.

"It wasn't like this with her. She just didn't respond to me like you do. I always had to take the lead, and even then she acted as if she was the one doing me a favor," he said, obviously embarrassed to be talking about his previous relationship.

Genevieve felt blood rush to her cheeks. Even talking about Stacey made her jealous. At the same time, she couldn't believe Stacey could have ever looked at this beautiful man, and not have wanted every inch of him.

Genevieve leaned forward, her breasts up against his chest, and kissed his cheeks, first one then the other. Then she brushed her lips against his. She leaned back, and ran her fingers along his jaw line and through his curly hair. His eyes focused on her, and a soft sigh escaped his lips. Her fingers tickled the ends of his light blond eyes lashes, and she rubbed her lips to his golden eyebrows. Genevieve bent in and nibbled his neck, and kissed his earlobe.

In a swift motion, Danny pulled her on his lap, and rested his head against her chest. She grabbed his hair with her fingers, and laid her cheek against the top of his head. He stared up at her, and their lips met with a ferocity she had never even felt with Joe. She could feel his desire and her own blood raced through her body, with a passion she knew would take over if they didn't stop.

Danny gently separated them, watching Genevieve, his breathing coming hard and fast. She nodded shyly, and slid off his lap to sit beside him. He grabbed her hand, and she rested her head on his shoulder. They sat like this, until they could catch their breath.

"We'd better stop, before we aren't able to," Danny whispered, squeezing her hand.

Genevieve laughed in agreement. She knew they shouldn't rush into things, but also knew she wouldn't be able to put off her own feelings for much longer. She had wanted Danny for too long, to be near him and keep saying no. Where did they go from here?

Danny read her mind, and glanced over at her, his eyes a sea of emotion, and quietly asked, "Baby, will you marry me?"

Genevieve's breath caught in her throat. Had he just asked, what she thought he had asked? She stared at him incredulously, her mouth dropping open. His blue eyes fixed on her face, and in that moment she knew what the future held. She wanted nothing more, than to wake up next to this incredible man every morning, and make love to him at night.

"Yes, I will," she said simply.

He grabbed her and started kissing her. His lips were so warm and welcoming; she didn't care what happened in the next moment. All the years of fighting to stay away had come to the end. Now, she could let her true feeling guide her way, and allow the man she had loved for longer than she really knew into her life. The walls came crumbling apart, making time stand still. He was where she wanted to be, where she needed to be.

Chapter Twenty-Six

The children took the news of their parents impending marriage to each other well. The boys, having been so young when each of the absent parents had disappeared from their lives, acted as if they expected Danny and Genevieve to get married all along. After all, it confirmed their brother theory. Becca's face showed a shadow of times lost, but she was happy to see her mother smiling again and planning for the future.

Since Danny hadn't had a ring when he proposed, they took a trip up to the Black Hills to pick one out. Genevieve still had her wedding and engagement rings from her marriage to Joe. She wasn't ready to part with them yet, so she and Danny picked out an emerald, set in a white gold

Claddagh ring, as her engagement ring. Although she wasn't ready to part with her rings from Joe, she decided to wear them on a necklace, and picked out a chain to match. Danny was so supportive of anything related to her marriage to Joe, which she found comforting, and even a little strange. She didn't feel that giving when it came to Stacey.

Danny called Stacey to let her know their news, but she acted as if she couldn't have cared less. He also had other business to talk over with her regarding Marcus, so he stepped out of the room, as not to upset Marcus. When he got off the phone, his face was splotched with red spots caused from held in anger. Genevieve rubbed his hand until he calmed down, but didn't ask him about the conversation. As far as she cared Stacey was a selfish woman, who didn't deserve such incredible guys like Danny and Marcus in her life.

Birdie practically flew out of her seat, when Danny and Genevieve showed her their engagement ring, announcing their upcoming wedding. She hugged Genevieve so hard, Genevieve thought she would smother. She begged to be allowed to plan their reception, which they were more than glad to have her do. One less thing to figure out.

Genevieve asked Becca to be her maid of honor, and asked Ben to escort her down the isle. Danny had few friends, certainly none close enough that he felt could be best man. Instead, he appointed Marcus to the job. Marcus beamed with pride at being Daddy's best man. They invited only their close friends and family, which amounted to about fifteen people, including those from Genevieve and Danny's work places. It was to be a small, intimate wedding, since they both had done the big weddings in the past. All they really wanted was to declare their love, and start their long-awaited life together.

Genevieve was in the kitchen making breakfast, when Danny came in from his truck. In a grand attempt at romanticism, they decided to not sleep together until they were married, so Danny stayed at his house and Genevieve at hers. Even if it meant Danny left at two in the morning, after a night of cuddling on the couch.

"Good morning, baby, how are you?" Danny asked, yawning as he poured a cup of coffee.

Genevieve slid over by him, and grabbed him around the waist. He bent to kiss her, as she smoothed a wayward curl on his head.

"Better, now that you are here. I missed you last night," she said, pouting slightly.

Danny winked, and kissed her earlobe.

"I just left like five hours ago, how much could you have missed me?"

"A lot. I couldn't sleep after you left. I kept thinking about where we should have the wedding... and the honeymoon," she emphasized honeymoon.

Danny raised his eyebrows, grinning.

"I don't know about the wedding, but we could have the honeymoon anywhere, and I'd be happy," he said, pulling her to him.

The heat between them was building daily, making Genevieve glad they had decided on a quick wedding. The way he made her feel reminded her of the heat which had passed between them daily at the greenhouse, during their college years. A perfect idea crossed her mind, and she gasped. Danny looked at her, alarmed.

"What is it, can't resist me that much?"

"No... well, yes... but no. I know where we can have the wedding! I just have to make a few calls," she said, bouncing excitedly against Danny.

She could tell her bouncing was having a detrimental

effect on their willpower, and stopped.

"Are you planning to tell me, or just get me hot and bothered, until I don't really care anymore?" Danny asked, laughing.

"The greenhouse! Let's get married at the greenhouse!" Genevieve exclaimed.

A funny nostalgic expression came over Danny's face, and the corners of his mouth turned up slightly in a faint smile.

"Gen, did that time at the greenhouse mean as much to you, as it did to me?" he asked softly.

Genevieve was taken aback by the question. Didn't he know how she had felt then?

"Oh, Danny, you have no idea! That year at the greenhouse with you was… incredible. Since that year, I would often mentally go back there when times got tough. You have always been a center for me, a friend, and yes someone I dreamed about," Genevieve said seriously.

"No more dreaming, baby, this is real and you are mine. I have been yours, longer than you know," he said, brushing a stray strand of hair out of her face.

They were interrupted by Becca, who walked into the kitchen, and groaned at the sight of them in each other's arms.

"Oh, get a room," she said, and grabbed a bowl out of the cabinet.

Danny chuckled, letting go of Genevieve.

"Okay, smartass," Genevieve replied sarcastically to Becca. "But last time I checked this is my house, and I own all the rooms!"

Becca looked over her shoulder at her mom, and rolled her eyes. She poured herself a bowl of cereal, and headed for the dining room. Then she stopped in her tracks and turned around. She set her bowl on the counter, an inquisitive look crossing her face.

"I never thought of this, but how are we going to fit five people in this house? Ben's room is already too small, as it is," she said, glancing up at the ceiling.

Genevieve had thought about this problem, as well, but didn't really have an answer.

"We're not," Danny replied simply.

Both women turned to look at him, a question in their eyes.

"Well, you know I bought a house outside town, near the state park. It's a huge farmhouse I'm fixing up. I was hoping we could all move out there."

Genevieve thought about it, and liked the sound of moving outside of town to a place she and Danny could make their own. She peered around the house she and Joe had started their life in together, and a twinge of sadness tugged at her heart. Her eyes rested on Becca, who by the looks of it was feeling that same twinge. Plus, Becca liked being in town and near college. This was the only house Becca had ever known her whole life. A smile crept across Genevieve's face, as she came to a solution.

"Becca, this house has been paid off for years, and it's a connection to your dad. Why don't you keep it?" she said, watching Becca's face widen in amazement.

"What do you mean *keep* it?"

"What I mean is, I will sign the papers over to you, and the house is all yours. You just have to pay the utilities and taxes."

Genevieve almost lost her balance, when her slightly taller daughter plowed into her for a hug.

"You have got to be kidding me, Mom! That's so awesome! So, when are you and the crew getting out of my house?" Becca asked, letting Genevieve go and helping her right herself.

Danny was laughing behind them. Genevieve rolled her eyes.

"Well, slow down there, Bec, I still have to get married. That is, if the groom doesn't back out on me," Genevieve teased.

Danny snagged the bottom of her shirt, and tugged her back towards him, as he leaned against the counter. Her body formed to his, and she laid her head back on him. Becca made a face of disgust, and left the room.

"Not a chance," Danny whispered deeply in her ear. "This is forever."

Genevieve basked in the moment, hearing Danny's heart beat against his chest. His body was a smooth tight support against her back, and her mind wandered into forbidden territory. She had seen and felt him with his shirt off before, but she wondered what it would be like to be intertwined with him... with nothing on, and no one around. A sigh escaped her lips, as she thought impatiently about the wedding. At least now they had a place. Or maybe that was still undecided. She turned around and faced Danny.

"So... the greenhouse?" she asked sweetly.

"Perfect," Danny said, and kissed her forehead.

The boys came running around the corner, chasing each other with squirt guns. Danny deftly disarmed them, and squirted each one of them for good measure. They squealed and jumped around. Even though they looked nothing alike, with Ben's red wavy hair and gray eyes next to Marcus's straight brown hair and green eyes, they were so similar in personality one could mistake them for brothers. Marcus unexpectedly ran up to Genevieve, wrapping his arms around her legs. She glanced at Danny, who shrugged giving her a lopsided grin.

"What do I call you?" Marcus asked her, peering up

from her legs.

Genevieve knew what he was talking about. Once she and Danny got married, should he call her Mommy? She had wondered and stressed over this as well, not wanting to ask too much, but still asking to be more than just Danny's wife to Marcus.

"That's up to you, Marcus, you call me what ever you are comfortable with," Genevieve replied, as she ran her fingers through his dark smooth hair.

Marcus put his lips together in deep thought, and then smiled.

"I think I will call you MeMe," he said happily.

Genevieve again looked at Danny for approval, and he nodded his head.

"Okay, Marcus, but why MeMe?" she asked.

"Because it's like Mommy, and you will never leave me," Marcus replied, with five-year-old logic.

Danny winced slightly, remembering the pain Marcus had suffered at Stacey's abrupt departure. Genevieve met his eyes, sending him a mental message she would never do that to them. His face relaxed, message received. Genevieve looked over at Ben, to make sure this wasn't going to cross any bonds, but he looked as if he couldn't figure out why this hadn't happened sooner. He trotted over to Genevieve and Marcus, and seemed puzzled.

"So, what do I call Danny?" he whispered, eyeballing Danny carefully.

Danny's face remained a blank slate.

"Duh, Ben, you call him Daddy," Marcus snorted, letting go of Genevieve's legs. He didn't understand Ben's dad was not his own.

Ben shook his head hard, and stared at his feet. Genevieve bent down, putting her hand on his shoulder. He looked up at her, with a sadness she hadn't seen in a long time.

"Ben, honey, you can just call him Danny. He isn't trying to replace Daddy," she said softly.

Ben bobbed his head, and wrapped his arms around her neck. Marcus, distracted by the television, ran out of the room to see what show was coming on next. Ben breathed into Genevieve's neck, making it tickle. He pulled his head back and looked at Genevieve seriously.

"Can I just call him Day? It's like Danny and sorta like Daddy. It's okay I guess," Ben whispered in Genevieve's ear.

Genevieve embraced him closely, fighting back the tears of pride she had for her brave, little son. Both of their boys had shown remarkable maturity in the changes in their life.

"Of course, Ben, that would be nice. I think Day is a very special thing to call Danny," she whispered back.

Ben let go of her neck, and dashed out to join Marcus.

"What was all the whispering about?" Danny asked curiously, from across the room.

Genevieve stood up and walked over to him. She grasped his hand, and gently pressed her lips to his knuckles.

"You are officially Day, and I am MeMe," she said, ceremoniously bowing.

Danny laughed, shaking his head.

"Day, huh? I could get used to the sound of that. Now, who am I to you?" he asked quietly.

"You, Daniel Jacob Kent, are my heart and soul," she answered, kissing him on the chin.

"It's about time you figured that out," Danny said, not kidding at all.

Chapter Twenty-Seven

The greenhouse was transformed into a magical wonderland. White Christmas-style lights hung in arches from the ceiling. Flowers in muted shades of ivory, lavender, and peach, lined the side counters, which were draped in ivory silk.

The center counters had been cleared, and the floor scrubbed to a gleaming finish. Chairs, covered with ivory silk, were lined on either side in rows of three. A matching runner ran down between the chairs, to an arbor decorated with green ivy and ivory roses, intertwined with baby's breath—to represent the children. It was a change to take one's breath away. All in a matter of hours, thanks to

Genevieve's old friend Maureen... and, of course, Birdie.

Genevieve slipped her sleeveless, tiered silk dress over her head. She had chosen to go with a champagne color, since she had already been married once in a white dress. The drape neck complimented her smooth neck, and the freshwater pearl necklace and earrings Danny had given her the day before, added just the right touch of accent to the outfit.

Becca pulled Genevieve's hair up into a French twist, with just a few tendrils left down for effect. Dehlia did Genevieve's makeup, in soft tones to compliment the dress. Lastly, Genevieve slipped on a pearl bracelet her grandmother had worn every day, and then given to Genevieve before she passed away. Genevieve had given her wedding rings from Joe to Becca for safe-keeping for the day, although she intended to give them to her one day for good.

After slipping on her crystal cascaded sandals, Genevieve rose to show Dehlia, Maureen and Becca her completed look. The three women gasped, their eyes wet with tears. Becca was the first to speak.

"Isn't it supposed to be the other way around, the mother crying at the daughter's wedding?" she said, trying to hold back the tears, so she wouldn't smudge her makeup.

Genevieve felt tears spring to her eyes, and bit her lip to stop them.

"Your day is coming. I promise, I will bawl loudly, and carry on for it, okay?" Genevieve insisted, to her stunning daughter, dressed in lavender chiffon.

Becca nodded, and grinned.

Genevieve couldn't believe this gorgeous creature standing in front of her, could possibly be her little Becca. Becca's waist length brown hair shined with rhinestones she had placed strategically throughout. Becca's tall slender body made the dress look even better than it had in the catalog. Genevieve secretly mused she might be upstaged by her own daughter. That was until she turned and glimpsed into the mirror in Maureen's office, where they were getting ready.

Her breath caught in her throat, as she looked into the glass, and saw the flushed, stunning woman staring back at her. If she was over forty, nothing reflecting back at her showed it. She looked like she was Becca's sister; the excitement of the day making her appear younger than she had in years. Her lips looked like plump berries, and her normally predominantly gray eyes shined with a green, which almost matched her engagement ring. Today she felt as youthful as Danny, and knew she would look perfectly matched next to her soon to be husband. Maureen came up behind her, smiling.

"Genevieve, I never would have thought the day I left Danny waiting in the greenhouse for you, it would come to this... so let's not leave him waiting in the greenhouse for you today. Are you ready?" Maureen asked, squeezing her arm.

Genevieve turned, and hugged her friend of so many years.

"More than you know," she replied, and took a deep breath.

Dehlia came up and placed her wrap over her arms. She kissed Genevieve on the cheek, smiling with a smile only another widow would understand.

"This is a day we all can only hope for, *twice* in a lifetime," she whispered, with tears in her eyes.

Genevieve nodded, and touched her friend's cheek.

"Your day will come again, you aren't meant to be alone the rest of your life," she whispered back.

"From your lips to God's ears," Dehlia said, as the three

women headed out, leaving Genevieve alone waiting on her escort.

A few minutes later, a soft knock came at the door and Genevieve answered it. Ben stood on the other side, looking handsome in his black tux. His red hair was brushed into soft waves, and he tugged uncomfortably at his tie. Genevieve felt a fresh wave of tears stinging at her eyes, and wondered if makeup had been such a good idea on this day.

Ben silently offered her his arm, which she took gratefully. There was no better person to walk her up the aisle. She gently clutched his arm with her other hand. He squinted up at her, and grinned. She grinned back, as she tried to quell the butterflies in her stomach.

It was only a short stroll to the greenhouse, but Genevieve became more and more nervous with each step. By the time they reached the doors, she felt nauseous and scanned for bushes, in case she needed them. At that moment, the doors opened and she saw Danny standing at the end of the greenhouse, and she knew she wouldn't. Her stomach settled in one swift second, at the sight of him. He simply took her breath away.

Danny stood with a delicate smile playing at the corners of his mouth, and his eyes fixed on her face. His face was such a calming presence; she didn't even notice the other people in the greenhouse. He was never more handsome, than at that very moment. His blond, curly hair was trimmed neatly, and almost glowed in the lights hung around the greenhouse. He was dashing in his tuxedo, causing Genevieve to hold her breath. As she walked down the aisle towards him, she felt as she was guided towards a beacon calling her home.

They came to the end of the aisle, and she bent down to kiss Ben on the cheek.

He smiled and said, "Go get 'em, Mom."

Genevieve chuckled, letting go of his arm. Ben sat down in the front row, as she turned to Danny. He gripped her hand in his own. Their eyes met, his a reassuring comfort. His hand was incredibly warm and solid around hers. They stepped forward under the arbor—Becca on one side, and Marcus on the other. The minister bowed at each of them.

Genevieve wished she could remember everything the minister had said, but her attention kept being drawn to the awesome man who stood beside her. Her eyes kept sliding over to watch him, her heart fluttering in her chest. From the way he clutched her hand, peeking over at her, she knew she was doing the same for him.

Then came the time they had to read their own personal vows to each other. Genevieve had chosen to go first, and turned to face Danny. She took a deep breath, and stared into his intense eyes.

"Danny, I can't explain the force you have been in my life. You have been my friend, my confidante, a pull I cannot ever put into words. You have waited on me, when you thought you would have to wait forever. In all the years, you never left my mind—I worried about you, cried for you, and hoped for you. Then, that day almost two years ago, I wanted to be with you. You let me try and figure out who I was, even when you should have given up on me. I cannot understand why God gave me not only one man who loved me with everything he had, but two to love me for life.

"I promise to give you all of me... for the rest of my life. When I look at you, I see home. I see a man who I was destined to be with, and a man I will not ever hurt intentionally again. I promise you my heart, and my love. I give to your son, Marcus, the same, and promise a home and a family he can count on. My heart and my soul are yours to depend on, and I will never run from you again. I stand here before you, and everyone present, with all humility to ask you to take me as I am. Give me shelter from the storms of life. I, in turn, will do the same for you," Genevieve stopped, placing her hand on Danny's cheek. "I lay myself bare before you, and give you everything I am."

Genevieve stared into Danny's eyes. His eyes were brimmed with tears, and he sniffed slightly with held back emotion. A stray tear slipped down his cheek. Genevieve gently wiped it away. He reached up and grabbed her hand, holding it to his chest.

"Baby, thank you, that's everything I could have ever hoped for and be offered," he paused to regain his composure. Finally, he went on, "First, let me say, before me stands a beauty I am honored to even look upon. You steal my heart away. I cannot believe you wanted me. I have wanted you for so long, the past and present blur into a fury of desire I can't even began to understand, much less form into words.

"I can tell you this. You will never want while you are with me. You will never fear. You will never need, or hurt, or wonder. With me you are safe from the world, and I will protect you with everything I have within me. I would lay down my life for you, and will spend the rest of my life letting you see how much I love you. You will never ever know loneliness again."

With this Danny kneeled down on one knee, and wrapped his arms around Genevieve's waist. He peered up at her, with an unhindered passion she had never seen in his eyes.

"Please take me as I am, humbled before you... a boy, a man... and love me as only you have ever been able to do.

I am yours forever… and in every way," Danny whispered, through tears.

Tears streamed unabated down Genevieve's face, and she questioned how she had ever been blessed to be loved by a man like this. She pulled Danny up and wrapped her arms around him, nodding, then murmuring, her answer. Not a dry eye was in the greenhouse, including the children, who knew that they had witnessed an exchange of love, which would affect their idea of what love should be—for the rest of their lives.

The minister finally cleared his throat, to bring back in to focus of the ceremony for the exchange of rings. Genevieve and Danny laughed bashfully, as they turned, blushing, towards the minister. The exchange of rings was a traditional one, although Genevieve's hands were shaking so badly Danny had to help her steady them, to slide the ring on his finger.

When he slid the ring on her finger, it felt as if it was more than just a piece of gold on her finger, but a flesh and blood connection to Danny. They clasped each others hands after the exchange, peering with disbelief into each other's faces.

All these years had finally culminated in a bonding of two people, meant to find each other. When the minister said that Danny could kiss the bride, Genevieve melted into him, and kissed him like she never had before. They ignored the whoops and hollers all around them, and forgot all time and space.

When they let their lips come apart, Genevieve was breathless, and marveled what their wedding night would bring. From the look in Danny's eyes, his thoughts were along the same line. He smiled at her timidly, as the minister announced them as husband and wife, and they headed back down the aisle.

Passage of Time

The reception was held at a hall at the college, and they danced the night away. Everyone in the newly formed family took turns dancing with each other, although Danny and Genevieve's took more turns together, than with anyone. Genevieve couldn't take her eyes off her new husband. When he came over to take her for a walk in the gardens, she was more than happy to oblige.

They strolled in silence in the chilly night air, until they came to the entrance. Noticing her shiver, Danny took off his tux jacket and placed it around her shoulders, followed by his arm. She snuggled in close, and breathed in the delightful smell of her husband. They walked the maze of the garden, arriving at the fountain in the center.

Danny turned Genevieve towards him and bent down, brushing his lips against hers. He wrapped his arms around her, pulling him into his warm space.

"Genevieve, there was a time in this garden you gave me a special gift, in the form of a watch. You gave me permission to be connected to my past without shame, and I blew the moment by chasing you away with a really, *really* bad decision. Today you connected yourself to my future, but in return I want to connect you to part of my past. I brought you here to ask you a very important question, and you don't have to answer it right away. Well, it's… I want you to adopt Marcus," he said quietly.

Genevieve was too stunned to even answer at first.

"But Stacey…" she stammered.

"…doesn't care." Danny finished.

Genevieve reeled back in shock. How could a mother not care? Danny clasped her hand, leading her to a bench. They sat down and he faced her, with a serious expression.

"That day… a few weeks ago, when I was speaking to Stacey on the phone, I asked her if she would consider letting you adopt Marcus. You know, since she hadn't seen him after she walked out, when he was three. She said some horrible things, but agreed to let you. As a matter of fact, she even sounded relieved. That's why I was so upset when I got off the phone. I thought she'd at least put up a fight, but she couldn't have cared less."

"Danny, if she doesn't want Marcus to be her son, then it's her loss and my incredible gain. I would be more than honored to adopt Marcus as my son! I have received two of the best gifts today—a husband and another beautiful son."

Chapter Twenty-Eight

Becca took Ben and Marcus back to her house after the reception, where she had agreed to watch them for a few days after the wedding. Danny and Genevieve went out to Danny's, and now Genevieve's, farmhouse for their long awaited honeymoon. Both of them had wanted to remain close to the children, agreeing the perfect place to spend the honeymoon was out in the country at the farmhouse. After all, it was only each other they were planning to look at.

They rode out to the country in silence, each lost in their own worlds. Genevieve still couldn't fathom not only spending time alone with Danny was going to be a reality for tonight, but also a reality for the rest of her life. This idea sent tingles of excitement through her; however, it also made her incredibly nervous. From the feel of Danny's clammy hand gripping her own, she knew the feeling was mutual. She smiled wobbly at him. He grinned back, squeezing her hand.

To try and quell her anxiety, Genevieve reflected back on the beauty of the wedding and the reception. Becca was especially gorgeous, and Genevieve had noted that Rogan couldn't take his eyes off of her. He had spent most of the night dancing with her. With the way he was pressing her to him, Genevieve knew he had more than friendship on his mind. She only hoped he wouldn't hurt Becca. Genevieve had seen the slew of girls who came and went from the nursery to see him, and knew he wasn't the most faithful guy. She recognized she had to let Becca live her own life... to make her own decisions, but sometimes that was easier in thought than to do.

The truck pulled into the driveway of the farmhouse, and Danny cut the engine. They both sat there, waiting on the other to make the first move. Genevieve could feel the butterflies in her stomach starting all over again, and held on tight to Danny's hand. Finally, he turned to her and laughed softly.

"Shall we?" he asked, melting her with those incredible blue eyes.

He opened his door when Genevieve nodded, and got out. Genevieve slid out behind him, still clutching his hand. He helped her with her gown, and then guided her up the stone path leading to the front door. Once they got to the door, her scooped her up in his arms, pushing the door open with his foot.

Inside he set her down, and kissed her firmly on the mouth.

"Welcome home, Mrs. Kent."

Danny led her to the couch, where Genevieve sat down,

while he got the fire started in the fireplace. He pulled some thick, soft blankets and pillows out, and laid them in front of the fire. When he went to the kitchen to get wine and glasses, Genevieve climbed over to the blankets and removed her shoes, rubbing her sore feet. Danny came back in with the glasses of wine, setting them on the hearth.

Genevieve sat on her knees, and motioned Danny to come over to her. He smiled, as he kneeled in front of her. The both leaned up on their knees, and wrapped their arms around each other. Genevieve bent forward and kissed him, tasting his salty lips. Danny let out a sigh, and pressed her closer to him.

She felt the rapidness of his heartbeat through his shirt, and a jolt of excitement shot through her. This time they didn't have to stop. Danny sat back and handed her a glass of wine, as he took a sip of his own. They silently drank their wine, appreciating each other. Danny reached out and caressed Genevieve's leg. His large hands were warm and soothing to her body. She anticipated feeling them all over.

Genevieve sat her glass down, and slid Danny's jacket over his shoulders. He shrugged out of it, and took off his tie. Genevieve unbuttoned the top four buttons of his shirt, and slid her hands inside over his chest. She pushed him back gently, and he rested back on the pillows.

Genevieve unbuttoned the rest of his shirt, and slid it down his arms and off. The sight of him shirtless made her breathless. She traced her fingers across his shoulders, and down his chest to his stomach. She must have tickled him slightly, because he tensed up and pulled her onto him, chuckling. Their lips met, and Genevieve could taste the sweet wine on his mouth. She teased his lips with her tongue. In one swift motion, he flipped her on her back, with him on top. He pressed his lips to hers roughly, yet, tenderly. She whimpered, clinging to him, not wanting to go too fast, and wanting to have him all the same.

Danny was the one to break the hold, sitting back to catch his breath.

"Baby, you make me want to consume you, and be taken by you, at the same time."

Genevieve sat up, and slipped her dress off over her head. Danny's eyes grew wide, and for just a second he seemed like a teenage boy on his first time. He leaned forward and kissed her shoulder, then grazed it with his teeth. He reached back and unclasped her bra, kissing her neck as it fell to the floor. Genevieve rested back on the pillows, her eyes half closed. Danny ran his large hands over her breasts, and stroked her neck. She felt his bare chest against hers, as he kissed each of her cheeks. He then delicately brushed her eye lids with his lips, and pressed his mouth to hers, his tongue softly tickling hers.

Her eyes fluttered open, as he sat back and took her hands. He pulled her up to a standing, and his long fingers slid her undergarments off. Genevieve nervously went to cover her stomach with her hands, but Danny stopped her hands, shaking his head no.

"Gen, all of you is beautiful to me. Don't hide yourself, I want to see every inch of you," he whispered, kissing her fingers.

Genevieve let her hands drop to her sides, as Danny let his eyes take in her body fully. He reached out and cupped her buttocks, pressing her to him. Genevieve slid her hands up and unfastened his pants. She gently slid them over his waist, and down to the floor. Danny stepped out of them, and pushed them aside with his foot.

As he stood there naked, Genevieve took a step back and gasped. He was just so incredibly gorgeous! She gazed at his long lean legs, and his tight behind. She ran her fingers over his firm stomach, and stepped in as close as she could get to him. She breathed in deeply, smelling his musky scent, and her body responded with a flood of heat.

"Thank you for waiting for me," she whispered softly.

He tipped her chin back, looking honestly into her eyes.

"I knew you would come back to me," he said simply.

Genevieve wrapped her arms around him, placing her hands on his back, and they sank to the pillows. As they pressed their bare bodies against each other, they knew they couldn't wait any longer. Danny laid her back gently and met her eyes with a primal desire only she could satiate. When they came together as one Genevieve gasped, as all of her longing and hoping found a place to rest. Danny buried his face in her neck, and she twisted her fingers into his golden hair. They moved together in a rhythm of ecstasy, and Genevieve understood she had never truly been loved like this before. She could feel him move inside of her, an unending need to unite.

She let Danny take her completely, as a tidal wave of bliss spread over her body. She cried out in release, as he rocked inside her. Together they rode the wave of rapture, holding onto one another for dear life. Danny held her forcefully, kissing her with unimaginable profoundness. As their eyes locked, they both knew that neither one of them had ever experienced a union so strong.

Danny lay beside Genevieve, and ran his fingers through her hair. She turned to look at him, intertwining her fingers with his. He enclosed her close to him, and put his arm around her protectively. She set her head on his chest, her eyes closing as she was settled by the beating of his heart.

"Genevieve, you are all of me. I can't live without you," he murmured into her hair.

She nodded slightly, and nibbled his neck.

"You will never have to."

Genevieve wasn't sure when they had dozed off, but she woke in the early hours of the morning. Danny was asleep next to her, and it was still pitch black out. She propped up on one elbow, watching the rise and fall of his chest. He seemed so serene sleeping, and the memories of earlier in the night sent a tingle through Genevieve.

She reached out and brushed her finger tips across his lips. His hand flew up, grabbed her fingers, and pressed them to his lips. Without saying a word he was on top of her, Genevieve feeling his desire. She nodded without saying a word, and in a flash they were intertwined, moving at a feverish pace. Her pleasure came quickly, as she grabbed his back and cried out. He didn't stop and a few moments later he groaned, whispering her name. He collapsed on her, and then rolled over with her on top of him. She rested on him, regaining her energy. She picked her head up to look at his face. His cheeks were flushed, and his eyes focused on her. She had never seen him more breathtaking. She slid up and nibbled his lower lip. He kissed her, grinning.

"Baby, I can't get enough of you. It has never been like this before," he said, and cuddled her in beside him.

Genevieve traced his lips tenderly, and smoothed his eyebrows.

"For me either, my Danny," she said truthfully.

He raised his eyebrows in surprise.

Genevieve nodded, "You do things to me that no one ever has."

"And I'm just getting started," Danny chuckled, and nipped her ear lobe.

A shiver ran through Genevieve, as she snuggled even closer to her husband.

The next time she woke, it was morning and Genevieve was starving. She heard Danny in the kitchen cooking, and she sat up stretching. She was sore from head to toe, but didn't care. She stumbled to the bathroom to freshen up. She took a quick shower and brushed her teeth, catching a glimpse of the well-satisfied woman in the mirror. She snickered, shaking her head, and went to the bedroom.

The week before the wedding, all her belongings were moved out to the farmhouse. She fished through a box, until she found a pair of jeans and a sweater. She was slipping them on, when she felt a pair of hands go around her waist. She spun around, as her sweater slipped over her head, and faced Danny. He was there in a pair of blue jeans and nothing else. She slid her hands over his chest and kissed his mouth. He responded quickly, and caught her lower lip between his teeth gently. Genevieve slipped back, snapping her pants before they came back off her.

Danny smirked at her. "Now, there's a concept... doing it in the bedroom," he said grabbing her, and throwing her on the bed.

Genevieve got a fit of giggles, and yanked him down on top of her. Obviously, Danny would be ready anytime.

"Not until you feed me!" Genevieve bargained.

Danny feigned disappointment, and then pulled her up.

"Ah, I live to please. I have waffles cooking, as we speak," he said, pinching her on the behind.

Genevieve slapped his hand, and darted down the hall towards the kitchen. By the time he got there, she was already eating one plain waffle with her hands. He grinned at her.

"Gen, you drive me crazy, you know? Even you eating that waffle, is about the most desirable thing I have ever seen."

"Well, if you feed me, I promise you can have me in every room of this house," Genevieve teased.

Danny went over and piled her plate as high as he could.

She grabbed his hand, and drew his face down to her mouth. She planted a sticky, sweet kiss on his lips.

Over the next few days, they did make love in every room of the house... sometimes twice. When they weren't exploring each other's bodies, they took walks along the isolated country roads, hand in hand. Genevieve ran her fingers through Danny's curly, golden hair every chance she could get. She remembered the days in the greenhouse, when her fingers ached to touch his hair. She couldn't believe now she could openly. Usually it led to much more fun excursions, too.

On the last day before the kids were due to arrive, they went down by the creek. It was pretty warm in Nebraska for early December, so they packed a lunch and some blankets. They sat down by the water, and talked about the upcoming Christmas. It would be their first together, the kids first together, and the first in the new home. Genevieve wanted to do an old-fashioned Christmas, and reminisced about the ones her grandma used to have. Danny was strangely quiet.

"Danny what is it? Did I say something wrong?" Genevieve asked.

Danny shook his head.

"No, it's not you. It's just Christmas. We didn't really do that when I was a kid. My parents never did much," he explained.

Genevieve's heart broke at the idea of a little boy not having Christmas. Her parents may have been less than attentive, but they always made sure there was Christmas. Genevieve stared down at the scar on Danny's arm, recognizing the physical scars were nothing compared to the emotional scars he carried.

"Danny, our children will always have Christmas. *You* will always have Christmas. Our family will always focus on love and joy," she said earnestly.

She reached out her hand, tracing his scar with her fingers. He stopped her hand and pressed it to the scar, as if her touch somehow healed the pain which was trapped inside.

She was choked up when she continued, "And you will never have to suffer like that again. I will never let anyone hurt you... ever."

Danny watched her with the face of a little boy, and rested his head on her lap. She ran her fingers through his hair, as a tear slipped down her cheek and landed on his face. He sat up touching where the tear had fallen. He looked into her eyes, and brushed her tears away.

"I love you, my Gen."

Chapter Twenty-Nine

Early Christmas morning, Genevieve slipped out of bed and down the hall, towards the living room. The house was quiet and dark; the excitement of the day had yet to tickle the boys awake. She peeked in on them in their shared bedroom. There had been plenty of room for them each to have their own, but they were adamant about having the same room. Marcus had climbed into Ben's bed sometime in the night, and they were sprawled out head to toe on Ben's twin sized bed. Genevieve afraid to wake them, smiled and left them be.

The living room was dim, so Genevieve clicked on the colorful Christmas lights, and sat back to admire the bright rainbow of colors they cast across the room. She pulled a pair of baby booties out of the pocket of her robe, quickly wrapping them in metallic silver paper. She ran her hand over her belly, and felt her heart skip a beat. Something she never expected was even possible had happened, and she hoped Danny would be as excited as she was.

Her thoughts were interrupted by the sound of four feet running down the hallway. Ben burst into the room, his red hair standing up in every direction. Marcus was right behind him, practically knocking Ben over when he stopped suddenly in awe of the sight before him. Presents were stacked up everywhere, under the biggest tree Genevieve could find. The boys looked at each other their eyes round, and started whooping and hollering. Genevieve knew she didn't stand a chance of stopping that speeding train, so she slipped into the kitchen to put water on for coffee.

Coming back into the living room, she saw Becca walk in yawning and stretching, her arms up above her head. Becca had stayed the night, knowing the boys would be up at the crack of dawn to open presents. She rolled her eyes, and threw herself down on the couch. The boys were just about ready to rip into the presents, when Genevieve gave them the *mom* look, which stops most children in their tracks. They slumped their shoulders, and sat down next to Becca.

The kettle started whistling loudly in the kitchen, and Genevieve ran back in to shut it off. The smell of the brewing coffee was magnificent! She pulled a large coffeecake and plates out of the cabinets, to have while they were opening presents. Her hands went protectively over her stomach, when she felt a warm body come up behind her. Danny slid his arms around her, and buried his face in her hair.

"This is perfect," he murmured.

He moved to her side, and grabbed a coffee cup. Genevieve looked at his endearing tousled appearance, and counted her blessings. Danny peered out of one eye at her and grinned, blowing her a kiss. Genevieve almost broke and told him her secret, but caught herself at the last minute. She wanted to make this memorable.

Danny poured them both coffee, and headed out to relieve the boys of their patience. Genevieve grabbed the coffee cake and plates, following closely behind him.

Ben was bouncing up and down on the couch, while Becca glared at him with disdain. Marcus just sat and stared at the enormous pile of presents. With a flick of his finger, Danny set them free. They ran over, tearing into the presents with fervor.

As long as it had taken to shop for the perfect presents, wrap them, and label them, it was over in a matter of minutes, or so it seemed. Soon, the boys were chattering endlessly, surrounded by their stack of presents. Becca was silent, staring in amazement at the gift her mother had given her. She stared at Genevieve, with her mouth hanging open.

"You are *giving* me Daddy's share of the construction company?" she finally squeaked out.

Genevieve nodded enthusiastically.

"Mom, this is too much!" Becca exclaimed.

"No, it's not. I have no need for the business and it's part of you. When Ben gets of age, I expect you to bring him in on the business, if he wants. I have already talked to Sam, and he was thrilled to have you come aboard after graduation. If you want to, that is," Genevieve explained.

"Oh, I want!" Becca exclaimed. She got up and hugged her mom firmly. "Thank you, Mom."

"What's this?" Danny asked, holding up the package Genevieve had wrapped that morning.

Passage of Time

Genevieve feigned ignorance, shrugging her shoulders, smirking. Danny saw his name written on the present, and sat down on the floor near Genevieve's legs. As he pulled the paper off, the booties fell out. He frowned for a minute, turning them over in his hands, trying to figure out what they meant. Becca gasped when she saw them, staring at Genevieve with surprise.

Danny looked up, his blue eyes incredulous, and raised his eyebrows in question at Genevieve. She nodded, and placed her hand over her stomach. Danny glanced back down at the booties, then up again. A huge smile spread across his face. He jumped up, grabbing Genevieve and sweeping her off the couch. She shrieked with laughter. Danny set her gingerly back down, and placed his large hand over her still flat belly.

"A baby? Our baby? Are you sure? How did this happen? When did you find out? Are you happy?" A stream of questions rolled out of his mouth.

"Let's see, yes a baby, our baby, I am sure, I found out two days ago, I think you know *how* it happened, and yes I'm happier than you know," Genevieve answered, never taking her eyes off of his.

He met her gaze, and their eyes locked. A million words passed silently between them. Danny placed his arms around her, pulling her to his chest.

"My mom, the baby making factory," Becca said, but not meanly from the couch.

The boys sensed the conversation had turned interesting, and had stooped chattering on their side of the room. Marcus stood up, with a serious expression on his face.

"Who's having a baby?" he asked softly.

Danny let go of Genevieve, and stepped over to where the boys were. He kneeled down in front of Marcus, and put his hands on Marcus's shoulders. Marcus waited patiently, looking intently at his daddy's face.

"MeMe and I are," Danny said honestly.

Marcus let his eyes flicker over to where Genevieve was standing, and then focused back on Danny's face.

"Will you still keep me then?" Marcus asked.

Genevieve's heart wrenched. Marcus still carried so much fear, from when Stacey walked out on him.

"Of course, Marc. You're my son. This baby is part of you too, and will be your little brother or sister—to help take care of," Danny explained.

Marcus eyes lit up when Danny said brother or sister, and he turned to Ben.

"If it's a boy, he can share our room," he said earnestly.

Ben nodded almost imperceptibly, and glanced at Genevieve for reassurance. She winked at him, and he winked back... well blinked, really. She knew he would be okay, and Becca... well, Becca was an adult now, so she would deal either way. From the look on Becca's face, she didn't have any issues.

Later, as the children were busy playing with their toys, and Becca had headed out to see Rogan, Danny and Genevieve snuggled on the couch together. Danny stroked his hand through her hair, with his hand over her stomach.

"Gen, thank you."

"For what?" she asked, lifting her head off his shoulder to see his face.

He had a faraway expression on his face, as he answered.

"For being you. For our family. For loving me."

"Those were all easy things to do. My life has never seemed so right, as it has since we figured out we belonged together," she said, running her fingers across his hand.

It was the truth. Genevieve felt like everything made sense, now that she had finally figured out where the path of life was supposed to be taking her.

When they dozed off on the couch, wrapped in each other's arms, Genevieve had a strange dream.

She was walking through an unfamiliar house. The sound of a baby crying was guiding her through a series of dark rooms. No matter how hard she searched, she couldn't find the room with the baby. She was becoming frantic searching, and started to cry. Turning, she saw a room she hadn't seen before, and the baby's crying stopped.

She pushed open the door to a small dingy room with a baby's crib on the far end. Fear gripped her heart, as she made her way across the room to the now silent crib. In the corner of the room a movement caught Genevieve's eye, and she peered over to see a small boy with blond, curly hair and dirty face, crouched in the corner. He appeared to be about three or four years old, and was staring with a horrified expression at the crib.

Genevieve looked back towards the crib, and walked slowly up to it. She peered over the railing and saw the lifeless body of a little baby girl, eyes open, staring off into space. Genevieve's heart pounded in her chest, as she reached forward, calling out to the baby.

"Emily! Emily!" she cried.

The baby lay there expressionless. Genevieve's tears rolled down her face, and splashed onto the baby's head. Suddenly, the baby gasped and looked at Genevieve. Emily stretched her chubby hands up for Genevieve, and gurgled. Genevieve scooped her into her arms, pressing the soft, blond, curly hair to her chest. Emily snuggled against her, and twisted her tiny hands into Genevieve's hair. Emily stared up at Genevieve, with an expression of love in her intense blue eyes.

Genevieve looked over to the little boy, crouched in the

corner, his eyes matching the baby's. She knelt down beside him, and handed him the baby. He peered up at Genevieve, with a lost expression. She patted the baby, Emily, and smiled at him.

"See? She is okay... everything is okay now," Genevieve said reassuringly.

The boy's face lightened, and he smiled down at the baby, holding her tight. Genevieve touched the boy's soft, curly head. He wrapped his arms around her, as she held both of them to her chest.

Genevieve awoke with a start, and caught her breath. Danny bolted upright, glancing around, startled. He looked at her with a worried expression, matching the one of the boy in her dream.

Instantly, the dream made sense to her, and she grabbed Danny's hand. Confused, he watched her for an explanation. Genevieve told him of her dream, and he fell silent. Tears stung at his eyes, making him appear so young and vulnerable.

Genevieve turned his face towards hers.

"I know our baby. I know what the dream meant," she said earnestly.

Danny met her eyes, and a tiny flicker of hope danced in them.

Genevieve continued, "Our baby is a girl, she is Emily. That is what we will call her."

Danny's voice sounded almost hoarse when he spoke, "Oh, Gen, it's perfect. She is our Emily."

Genevieve climbed over on Danny's lap and laid her head on his shoulder. He reached around and covered her with his arms. The reality of second chances sank in... nothing else needed to be said between them.

"Emily Jo," Danny said, out of the blue, later on that day.

Passage of Time

Genevieve turned her head in question to him. Danny nodded his head and smiled slightly.

"Our baby. She is Emily Jo."

Chapter Thirty

The nursery was a dazzling array of pigs and elephants, dancing across the border and bedding. Six-week-old Emily watched her mobile twirl intently, her blue eyes as big and beautiful as her daddy's. Everything about Emily looked like her daddy, from the top of her golden, curly head, to the tips of her long toes. She was a mini version of Danny, and thus a replica of her namesake.

The moment she had arrived, Danny and Genevieve had taken one look at her, then at each other, and had known that Genevieve's dream had been right. Danny had cried that day, holding his tiny daughter in his arms, and remembering his sister, who he had once held just that way. The circle had been closed.

Passage of Time

Today was a very special day. It was the day Danny and Genevieve were going to introduce their daughter to their friends. Rather than a baby shower while Genevieve was pregnant, they had decided it was more fitting to have everyone come out to the farmhouse, when Emily was ready to be introduced to the world.

There was also another very special person for Genevieve to introduce, as well, today. The final adoption papers had just come through last week, and today she would introduce Marcus as her son. Danny had sat the boys down one day, to ask their feeling about Marcus being adopted by Genevieve. Both of them had grinned, with that knowing look. After all, all along they had known they were really brothers. It was as if they had waited for their parents to arrive at that awareness.

Marcus didn't really remember Stacey, so he seemed anxious and excited about being Genevieve's son. Over the months he had stopped calling her MeMe, and started calling her Mommy.

However, Ben remembered his father and had no interest in being adopted by Danny. He and Becca both loved Danny, and felt he was like a father, but they wanted to remain Joe's children in heart and name. Neither Danny nor Genevieve had a problem with that. By Emily and Marcus being both their children, there were enough blood bonds to go around, connecting all of them.

Genevieve scooped Emily up out of the crib, burying her nose in Emily's springy hair. Emily instinctively reached forward and grabbed on to the ends of Genevieve's hair, holding on tightly. Genevieve laughed and hugged her tiny daughter close. She couldn't believe how blessed she was to have four children to call her own. It was the big family she had craved when she was just a small, and only, child.

The doorbell rang, signaling their first guest. Genevieve

finished buttoning up Emily's light blue dress, and ran a comb through her unruly hair. She laughed, thinking if Danny let his hair grow, he would have this kind of haphazard curly, blond hair too. He tended to keep it cut pretty close to his head, so it formed soft golden waves.

Speaking of, Danny walked in and took Emily from Genevieve's arms, bending to kiss his wife. She leaned up, hugging the both of them. Danny was making silly faces at Emily, who just stared back at him weirdly. Genevieve ran to get the door, leaving them standing in the nursery, with Danny blowing raspberries on Emily's neck.

"About time!" Maureen laughed, as Genevieve swung the door open. "Thought I had the wrong day, or the wrong house... stuck out in the middle of nowhere."

"Right day, right house, slow host," Genevieve said, snickering as she let Maureen in.

Maureen whistled as she glanced around the living room. They had done a lot of work, and brought some culture into the worn house. Ben and Marcus raced through, chasing each other and hollering. Maureen turned and grinned at Genevieve.

"Never a dull moment, huh? Who knows, maybe Jack and I will have a houseful," Maureen said wistfully.

She had recently married another of the professors at the college. Although he had children from a previous marriage, Maureen had never been married before, nor had any children. At forty-two she knew her chances were getting slimmer.

"Speaking of the baby, how is it having a crier in the middle of the night again?" Maureen asked.

"Oh, Danny? He's alright, more of a weeper, really," Genevieve replied, winking. "As for the baby, by the time she is ready to eat, Danny already has gotten her, and has brought her to me!"

"Wow, well trained husband. Have to get some tips on that one," Maureen kidded.

Genevieve laughed, but secretly something about Danny's midnight radar had always left her unsettled. It was as if he was afraid of something. He was getting dark circles under his eyes from the lack of sleep, waiting for Emily to stir. Genevieve pushed it out of her mind, as Jack came sauntering in, carrying Maureen's purse.

Jack was at least Maureen's age, but a distinguished gray, while Maureen battled aging with every product on the market. Genevieve knew that under Maureen's shimmering blond hair was gray, just waiting to burst through. Her own hair was getting a little gray; although it just made her auburn hair just appear lighter, more golden. She wasn't ready to break out the bottle of color... yet.

The doorbell rang again, and this time Dehlia was bending over, trying to keep Roderick from messing up his hair, as Genevieve opened the door. Dehlia looked up and rolled her eyes, giving up as Roderick rubbed his hands through his hair. He had grown into such a handsome little boy, and buzzed past the both of them to find Ben and Marcus, who were making a ruckus on the other side of the house. Genevieve took Dehlia's sweater and hung it in the closet.

"Is Bobby coming today?" Genevieve asked, referring to Dehlia's boyfriend.

Dehlia shook her head, and sighed.

"No, and he's never coming. We broke up. I just don't need another boy, not ready to be a man."

"Oh, I'm sorry, Dehlia! The right man is out there, sifting through all the loser girls, to try and find his woman too," Genevieve said.

Dehlia shrugged and smiled.

"Yup, and he'd better be ready to step up to the plate

233

when he finds me!" She kissed Genevieve on the cheek, and made her way over to Maureen.

They started chatting, as the front door was thrown open to reveal Becca and Rogan standing there, with a huge cake in their hands. Genevieve was surprised to see Becca with Rogan again. They had been almost inseparable the past year, but Genevieve still had a bad feeling about Rogan with her daughter. Becca made a face of impatience to Genevieve.

Genevieve chuckled, and took the cake from Becca's hands. It read "Danny, Genevieve, Becca, Ben, Marcus, Emily" in a circle. In the middle of the names it read "Our Family". Genevieve sniffed emotionally, setting it on the table. Birdie arrived shortly after, with containers full of food she didn't need to bring, but insisted on bringing anyhow.

Soon, all the guests had arrived, and had started eating. Once she could see everyone was settled in, Genevieve pulled Danny aside to hand him a present she had made. He looked at her with a confused smile, and opened it. He stared down at the picture, wordless. Genevieve was afraid she had crossed the line by having it done, and started to apologize when Danny spoke.

"Damn, baby, just when I think you could have given me every possible gift... you think of something else," he whispered.

"I hoped you wouldn't mind. I found that picture you had tucked away, of your sister, and had it restored and blown up. I just thought, she is part of our family, and there needs to be a picture displayed of her in our house," Genevieve explained.

Danny bobbed his head, and pressed the picture to his chest. He set it on the mantle, and wrapped his arms around Genevieve. Nothing else needed to be said.

Passage of Time

Their Emily, tired of being handed around to all the guests, squawked—breaking their moment. They stared at each other, laughing. Genevieve went over and picked up Emily, as she got the attention of everyone in the room.

"Hello! Thank you all for coming to our special day. As I can see, everyone has become acquainted with our daughter, Emily, who needless to say let's her likes and dislikes be known!" A ripple of laughter went around the room. "Today is Emily's welcome party, but also today is special for another reason. Marcus, can you and Ben come up here? You too, Becca."

The children made their way up to the front of the room. Becca came and stood beside Genevieve. The boys stood in front of her, making faces at the guests. Genevieve tried her best to fight back the tears, which were stinging at her eyes. She took a deep breath, and went on.

"Not many of you know this, but at our wedding, Danny asked me to adopt Marcus. Adoption is never a quick process, just last week we were given the final papers, which made it official. Marcus is now truly my son, a place he has held in my heart for a long time," Genevieve said, as the tears she had been holding finally broke their way through.

Marcus gazed up at her, eyes wide with disbelief.

"Is it true, Mommy?" he asked incredulously.

Genevieve nodded, and put her hand on his head.

He turned around grabbing her legs.

"I have a real mommy, you hear that, Ben?"

Ben and Becca both stared, realizing that not only was Marcus Genevieve's son, but he was really their brother as well. Becca rubbed her nose, and peered down with wet eyes. Marcus went over to where Ben and Becca were standing, and jumped up and down. Ben looked at him, a huge grin lighting his face.

Becca kneeled down, and wrapped her arms around Ben and Marcus. She mouthed the words "thank you" to Genevieve and Danny. Ben broke away, and ran over to Danny.

"Thank you, Day! You gave me my brother for real. I love you, Day!" he said, and hugged Danny as hard as he could.

Although he had always been nice and respectful of Danny, Ben had always kept a safe distance. Danny glanced at Genevieve, his eyes shadowed with emotion. She smiled back, wiping her cheek. She glanced around the room, and saw tears were being shed all over. They would really have to have a get-together without so much emotion next time around.

Becca slipped up beside her, and handed her a small item. Genevieve peeked down at the item, seeing it was the ring Becca had given her on the anniversary of Joe's death. She thought she had misplaced it at the nursery, when repotting plants. In addition to Joe's, Becca's, Ben's, and Genevieve's birthstones, had been added Danny's, Emily's, and Marcus's birthstones. Genevieve gasped and met Becca' eyes. Behind her daughter's sarcasm, hid a heart of gold. She slipped the ring onto her hand, and closed her fingers around it.

The emotion of the day wore them out, and by the time the last guest had left, they were all ready to bed down. Genevieve nursed Emily, and put her in her crib. Emily yawned, and fixed her eyes on the mobile above her bed. Genevieve wound it up, watching her tiny daughter for a minute. Danny came in behind her, putting his arm around her waist, as he rested his chin on her shoulder. Emily's eyes started their drift towards dreamland.

Danny took Genevieve's hand, and led her to their bedroom. As they passed the boys' room, they saw them sound asleep in one bed... as usual.

Danny kissed Genevieve gently when they got to their bedroom, and slipped her dress off her shoulders. She sighed, and pressed in towards him. In all their time together, she never tired of feeling his hands on her. She ran her hands up his back, and into his hair.

Danny led her to the bed, and laid her gingerly back. He kneaded her shoulders, and massaged her body head to toe. Genevieve couldn't ignore the yearning she felt for him, and pulled him down on top of her, her body arching to be one with his. He looked at her for reassurance, as they had not made love since Emily was born.

Genevieve bent forward, and caught his earlobe between her teeth, whispering fervently, "Yes."

They came together in a desperate need to remind themselves it all started with just them. Danny held her tenderly, and murmured his love into her ear. He took his time, touching her everywhere, making her body cry out in desire.

Genevieve brushed her lips against his, and crushed her mouth to his, needing to possess all of him. She moved with him, matching every stroke, and called out his name as he brought her to her limits. Afterwards, he pulled her to him, wrapping himself around her like a blanket. She knew she would never have to crave again.

Later that night, she woke to hear Emily fussing in her crib. She glanced over at Danny, who had never not awoken first for Emily, and saw his exhausted face deep in sleep. She smiled, and slipped out of bed. By the time she got to Emily's room, the baby was fussing more, and threatened to start squalling. Genevieve quickly unbuttoned her nightgown, and reached for Emily just as she hit melt down.

As she sat down and put Emily to her breast, Danny

came rushing to the door, scaring Genevieve, making her and the baby jump. She stared into Danny's panic-stricken face, like the face of the terrified boy in her dream. All the pieces fell into place. Danny was getting Emily, because he was afraid to lose her. He was afraid to see another mother take the life of her child.

"Come here, baby," Genevieve whispered, putting her hand out to Danny.

Like a child, he came and sank down at her knees. She rubbed his head, and he rested it on her knees. Pain racked his body, as Genevieve ran her fingers down his neck, and through his hair.

"She's okay, everything will be okay now," Genevieve repeated the words from her dream.

Danny's gripped her legs like a vise. So much pain and fear poured out of him, as he let Genevieve soothe his soul. He peered up, eyes red-rimmed, and focused on Emily.

"I have just been so afraid. I did this with Stacey, too," he confessed. "I almost kept Marcus away from her.... no wonder she left, I never let her bond with him. And now with you, the person I trust more than life itself. I just have been so afraid."

Genevieve took in his words, and knew it was time for healing for both of them. She supported Emily at her breast with one hand, and placed her hand on Danny's cheek with the other. Their eyes met and locked. A lifetime of understanding passed between them. The shadows in his eyes passed, and left was a clear blue, with no hint of the pain which he had carried for so long.

"I promised you, that I would never hurt you again. That promise carries to every part of you... Emily and Marcus included. You, and they, are safe with me. My love for you is what my love for them is. You will never have to worry or suffer again.

238

Passage of Time

I am your *forever*, and you are mine. It's time for us to let go of those things which haunt us. This time belongs to no one else.

This is our time."

About The Author

Have you ever noticed how the *about the author section* is usually written by someone other than the author? And it really doesn't tell you anything about the author. Seriously, do you really care if I have cats or not? (I don't, but if I did would it matter?)

This is what I think you should actually know about me:

I don't function without my morning cup of coffee. Well, I do, but not well and am a real pain in the butt without it. Better off with it!

I have a temper. It takes awhile to set off, but when it goes I am totally unreasonable. Just ask anyone who knows me… hmm, although they may lie to avoid setting me off!

I sing in the car. I couldn't care less if anyone sees me, after all everyone *wants* to sing in the car, but are too afraid to look stupid. I gave up on not looking stupid a long time ago.

I like wine and pizza. Together, apart, doesn't really matter. I like cookies, too (who doesn't?). Lima beans I could live without.

I can grow plants outside, but not in my house. Don't know why. Walking through those doors is the kiss of death for any plant. I can almost hear them scream crossing the threshold.

In my life, I have lived all over the US and one place outside. I love something from every place I have been, especially the food! I love food, comfort or otherwise.

If I could sing better, I would have been a rock star...er, well, maybe only in my fantasies. I really can't play an instrument well, and hate standing in front of groups. But if the shower and lip synching count, I rock!

Thank you for reading my story, and getting to know Danny and Genevieve. They are as much part of my family, as the flesh and blood members. Now, if I could only stop referring to my husband as "Danny". Just kidding.

Now you know all about the author!

Sissy

Books by DogTag Publishing

Children's Fiction:

No Matter What: A Tribute to a Child Lost
by Julie Doggett

Families Are Families Forever
by Julie Doggett

Adult Non-Fiction

Peering Out Through the Cracks:
Coping on the Inside
by Juliet Freitag

Adult Fiction

Passage of Time
by Sissy de Grace

Books can be ordered through:
www.dogtagpublishing.com
and various online booksellers.